ALAN JUDD

DEEP BLUE

**SIMON &
SCHUSTER**

London · New York · Sydney · Toronto · New Delhi

A CBS COMPANY

First published in Great Britain by Simon & Schuster UK Ltd, 2017
A CBS COMPANY

1 3 5 7 9 10 8 6 4 2

Simon & Schuster UK Ltd
1st Floor
222 Gray's Inn Road
London WC1X 8HB

www.simonandschuster.co.uk

Simon & Schuster Australia, Sydney
Simon & Schuster India, New Delhi

A CIP catalogue record for this book
is available from the British Library

Paperback ISBN: 978-1-4711-5065-4
eBook ISBN: 978-1-4711-5066-1

Typeset in the UK by M Rules
Printed and bound by CPI Group (UK) Ltd, Croydon, CR0 4YY

MIX
Paper from
responsible sources
FSC
www.fsc.org   FSC® C020471

Simon & Schuster UK Ltd are committed to sourcing paper that is made
from wood grown in sustainable forests and support the Forest Stewardship
Council, the leading international forest certification organisation. Our
books displaying the FSC logo are printed on FSC certified paper.

Praise for Alan Judd

'Plotting in the best le Carré tradition'
Mail on Sunday

'Belongs to the classic tradition of spy writing'
Guardian

'Judd infuses his writing with insider knowledge'
New Statesman

'Wonderful. One of the best spy novels ever'
Peter Hennessy on *Legacy*

'Entertaining and compulsively readable'
Melvyn Bragg on *A Breed of Heroes*

'John le Carré has no peer among contemporary spy novelists,
but Judd is beginning to run the master close ...'
Daily Mail

'Judd is a masterful storyteller, with an intricate knowledge
of his subject and a sure command of suspense'
Daily Telegraph

'Rivetingly accurate'
Observer

'Alan Judd writes exceedingly well'
Evening Standard

'Judd keeps plot and action centre-stage ... he has written a
novel perfect for brightening up a drizzly winter Sunday'
Mail on Sunday

'This is undoubtedly Judd's best spy novel yet – both as
a thriller and in terms of its plot construction'
Spectator

'He knows that world backwards and writes with an
understanding of human frailty that is rare'
Sunday Express

Also by Alan Judd

Fiction
A Breed of Heroes
Short of Glory
The Noonday Devil
Tango
The Devil's Own Work
Legacy
The Kaiser's Last Kiss
Dancing with Eva
Uncommon Enemy
Inside Enemy
Slipstream

Non-Fiction
Ford Madox Ford (biography)
*The Quest for C: Mansfield Cumming and
the Founding of the Secret Service* (biography)
First World War Poets (with David Crane)

To Derek Hillier

Chapter One

The Present

Agent files – paper files, anyway – told stories. It was never quite the whole story – nothing was ever that – and they could be misleading, repetitive and elliptical, but as you opened the buff covers and fingered the flimsy pages of carbon-copied letters and contact notes, and the thicker pages of Head Office minutes or telegrams from MI6 stations, a skeleton became a body and eventually a person. It was the story of a relationship; sometimes, almost, of a life. And sometimes, as with the file that Charles Thoroughgood sat hunched over that evening, it bore the ghostly impress of another story, an expurgated presence that had shaped the present one without ever being mentioned.

Files rarely lied in terms of content; their lies were usually by omission, nearly always on security grounds. In this case Charles knew those grounds well, having written much of what was in the file, and nearly all of what wasn't, many years before.

1

Pellets of rain splattered against his office window, invisible behind the blinds he had insisted upon despite assurances that the security glass could not be seen through. Having spent much of his operational career penetrating the allegedly impenetrable, he was reluctant to accept blanket security assurances. The more confident the assertion, the less he trusted it, and now, as Chief of MI6, he was better able to assert his prejudices than at any point in his eccentric and unpredictable ascent to the top. But not as much as he would have liked; Head Office was still in Croydon and the government seemed in no hurry to fulfil its promise of a return to Whitehall.

He was on volume three of the file, the final volume, reading more slowly as he neared the point where he had joined the case as a young officer on the Paris station during the Cold War. He was alone in the office but for the guards and a few late-stayers, having sent his private secretary home. Sarah, his wife, was also working late, the common fate of City lawyers. The file was a relief from his screen with its unending emails and spreadsheets; also an escape into a world which, because it was past, seemed now so much simpler and clearer than the present. But it had seemed neither simple nor clear then.

There was no hint of a link to another file, no reference to papers removed. When at last he found what he sought he moved the green-shaded desk lamp closer and sat back in his chair, the file on his lap. Movement reactivated the overhead lights, which he disliked for their harshness, but if he stayed still for long enough they would go out. The desk lamp he had brought in himself, against the rules.

The paper he sought was in two sections, the first typed in Russian in Cyrillic script, the second a translation into English by someone from the Russian desk in Century House, the old Head Office during much of the Cold War. They should not have been in this file at all, an ordinary numbered P file belonging to a dead access agent run by the Paris station. Josef, as Charles had known him, was a Russian émigré who, unusually, had been allowed out of the Soviet Union on marrying a secretary from the French Embassy. Before that he was a journalist who had committed some minor indiscretion which had earned him ten years in a labour camp, in the days when ten years was what you got for being available to fill a quota, especially if you were Jewish. Settled in France, he had come to the notice of the Paris station, which had recruited him to get alongside visiting Russians. The relationship with the Secret Intelligence Service lasted many years, sustained by snippets from Josef which usually promised more than they delivered, and by payments from SIS, before Charles was sent to terminate him. That was when the case became interesting.

The paper did not, in fact, pertain to Josef at all, though that would not have been apparent to anyone reading the file. It was recorded that Josef had been in a labour camp, so a first-person account of a visit to the camp years after it had closed would be assumed to be his. The account had been left on Josef's file after other papers had been silently removed, doubtless because whoever weeded the file had made the same mistaken assumption. By the time Charles had discovered it, both Josef and Badger, code-name of the author of the paper, were dead. It might have drawn attention to the Badger case to have transferred papers to it years later. Not that anyone read old paper files any more. Charles was probably the only person still serving who knew both cases.

There was no real need for him to re-read Badger's account of his visit to his former prison camp. Charles remembered it well enough and his renewed interest in the case now, so many years later, was not because of that. He read it partly because he was nostalgic, partly to revive his sense of the man known as Badger, whose own file he had yet to re-read, and partly in penance, acknowledgement of unfulfilled promise. The description of the camp visit was intended by Badger to be part of the memoir he never wrote, an indication of what he hoped to publish when safely resettled in the West. But he never was resettled and this was the only chapter written. Charles had promised that, if anything happened to Badger, he would see it published somewhere. And never had.

Turning to the typewritten English translation, marked by Tippexed alterations and the translator's margin comments in pencil, Charles read:

Since I was in that remote region, the region of my last camp, and with time to spare before the flight back to Moscow, I told my driver to take me to it. He was puzzled. 'There's nothing there, it was closed years ago. Just the huts and the wire and some of the old guards who have nowhere else to go.'

'Take me.'

It was farther from the airport than I thought and there was fresh snow, unmarked by other car tracks. It was fortunate that the driver knew the way because I should never have found it, hidden in a clearing in the midst of the forest. The iron gates were open and, judging by the depth of snow piled up against them, had been so since autumn. The grey sky was breeding more snow now and on either side the high outer fence stretched into the blurred distance, sagging in places. The watchtowers stood like tall black cranes, one of them with a dangerous list. Inside the wire, the huts were squat white shapes with here and there a misshapen one where the roof had collapsed. The doors at the ends, shielded by overhangs, were mostly shut but some sagged open on rotted hinges.

I told my driver to wait and keep the engine and heater running. Then I walked slowly through the gates. There were other footprints in the snow leading to the first hut, a larger H-shaped one which used to be the guardroom. Behind it was the inner fence with another set of open gates. Within that fence were the huts. The guardroom door opened before I reached it. I wasn't surprised. The sight of a shiny black ZiL and an official in a long black overcoat with a sable astrakhan and matching gloves was not a common one for the wretches within. A hunched figure hobbled out, muffled in old clothes and using a stick. He hurried over as if afraid to miss me.

'Greetings, greetings, I am Kholopov, Ivanovich Kholopov. I was sergeant here. I am your guide, if you wish.'

He had a thin dirty face and his lips were never still, working continuously. He looked smelly. I knew he would be, I knew exactly how he would smell, but I had no need to get that close.

'I know the camp well, I know everything about it, I have been here nearly thirty years. I worked here, I was sergeant of the guards.'

I took off one glove and fished out a few coins from my coat pocket. I didn't bother to count them. He held out his hand, his glove worn through on the palm, and I dropped them into it without touching him.

'Thank you, thank you kindly. What would you like to see – the kitchen, the offices, the punishment cells, the graveyard, the huts, the bathhouse? It is all empty, all available.'

'Everything. Show me everything.'

That puzzled him. 'Of course, of course, I can

show you every hut, every bunk. Only there are very many and it will take time—'

'I will tell you when to stop.' I noticed now that he had a twitch in his left cheek.

'With pleasure, it is pleasure. Please follow me.'

We crunched through the snow together, slowly because of the curious way he hobbled. He told me about the building of the camp in the 1930s, initially by the first prisoners sent to it who lived – and often died – in holes in the ground until the huts were up. He described its expansion, then its gradual contraction after the death of Stalin until its closure in the Gorbachev era, by which time it housed only a few politicals, as he called us.

'But when Comrade Gorbachev let the prisoners go the authorities forgot about us, the guards and administrators. We stayed, we had nowhere to go. How can we go anywhere? Where could we go? There is no work for us here but we cannot afford to move. Unless they open the camp again.' His laugh became a prolonged cough. 'We have pensions but they are a pittance, which is why we have to beg from generous visitors such as yourself.'

We reached the first of the huts inside the inner wire. The number one was still just visible in faded white on the wooden door. 'We can go in if you want but there is nothing there, nothing to see. They're all the same. In this block there are numbers one to thirty-nine, the rest are in the other block.

Twenty prisoners to a hut but sometimes there were more. They are all the same, the huts. So were the prisoners. Over there are the camp offices and the punishment cells and the bathhouse and the sick bay and our own quarters. They are more interesting. These are just huts.'

I offered him a cigarette. He glanced as if to check that he had not misunderstood, then grabbed one. 'Thank you, thank you.' His eyes lingered on the packet, which he couldn't read because they were American, Peter Stuyvesant. His eyes lingered too on my gold lighter. 'Number thirty-seven,' I said. 'Take me to thirty-seven.'

The cigarette seemed to give him energy and his lop-sided hobble through the rows became more rapid. The smoke was good and pungent in the cold air.

'You see, they are all the same,' he said again when we reached it.

'Open it.'

I sensed he was reluctant, probably because of the effort involved. He put his cigarette between his lips, leaned his stick against the wall, pushed down on the handle and put his shoulder to the door. It was obviously stiff at first but then opened so freely that he nearly lost his balance. He stood back so that I could look in. 'Nothing to see, just the bunks. They're all the same.'

He had to move as I stepped in. It took a while for my eyes to adjust to the gloom. There were sprinklings of snow on the earth floor beneath the closed wooden window-hatches. The ceiling was low, the wooden double bunks lined the sides, some with broken slats, others still with remnants of old straw. The gangway down the middle was too narrow for two to walk side by side and to get between the bunks you had to go sideways. There was an old metal bucket on the floor by the door and a musty smell. It felt colder inside than out.

I walked two-thirds of the way down and stopped by the lower bunk on the left side. It was no different to all the others, of course. My guide hobbled behind me.

'You knew someone who was here?' he asked.

I didn't answer. After another minute or so of fruitless and circular contemplation, I turned back up the aisle. You live with the past but you can't live it. I left my guide struggling to close the door and headed back towards the gates. The snow was thicker now and the outlines of distant huts rapidly became indistinct. Eventually I heard him shuffling and panting and he caught up with me.

'Is there anything else – the punishment cells, the camp offices?'

I was between the inner and outer fences, approaching the H-shaped guardroom, when he made one last effort, pointing with his stick. 'I could show you the cookhouse. We use it. It still has the ovens and pots and pans—'

That made me stop and think. 'No,' I said. 'That was the guards' cookhouse. The cookhouse for the prisoners was that one, there.' I pointed at a long low building just inside the inner fence.

He followed my gaze, then looked back at me, his lips still for once. 'You are right. I had forgotten. I have been here too long, I am too familiar. But you, how could you—'

'I was here.'

We stared at each other in a long silence, but for the hiss of the snow. Those three words, three simple words, sunk into him like stones in a pond. Who were the prisoners, the real prisoners? And how could I be a senior official with a ZiL and furs? I took the cigarettes and the remaining coins from my pocket. He dropped his stick in the snow and held out his cupped hands. He was still staring, uncomprehending, as my car pulled away.

At the foot of the original Russian text was a handwritten note in English, in Badger's characteristic forward-sloping hand and his usual brown ink: *So you see, Charles, we are all prisoners really, even the guards. Tell your people who doubt my motivation – is this not enough?*

Charles closed that volume of Josef's file and put it with its mate. Then he picked up Badger's file, a slim single volume also buff-coloured but this time with a red stripe, a different number system and a white stick-on label with heavy black lettering saying, 'Closed. Do not digitise.' He had stuck that on himself years before, proof of rare premonition. It meant the case had remained secret and, unlike digitised files, was fully recoverable.

Chapter Two

The Present

'But I thought you'd have been back ages ago, before me. That's why I left the message about the fish, so that you could be getting on with it.' Sarah closed the oven door with unnecessary force. 'If I'd known you were going to be so late I could have stayed and finished what I was doing.'

'Sorry. I thought you were going to be later so I just carried on.'

'You could've let me know. And now it's gone ten and neither of us has eaten. It's ridiculous. It's not good to eat so late. Medically, I mean.'

'Mexicans do.'

'Bugger the Mexicans.' She had to stop herself smiling. 'I think you enjoy provoking me, don't you?'

'Keeps you young.' He ducked the oven glove she threw. 'Chardonnay or Sauvignon?' In just over a year of marriage they had never had a row. They had tiptoed round each other, careful not to provoke, each watchful to see where the limits might be, aware that their being together at all was an unimaginable bonus. They had met decades before, as students, an intense relationship whose disintegration had had consequences as unimaginable as their present state. She had gone on to marry one of Charles's friends, who had preceded him as Chief of MI6. The events leading to his death had brought them together, events which could still make their new-found unity feel fragile. Whenever tension threatened, they almost competed to defuse it.

Over dinner, she said, 'I've just avoided a case we would both find embarrassing. Representing the Action Against Austerity movement in a human-rights case against the government. They've got some very left-wing barristers involved and I got out of it by arguing that it's really one for our litigation department rather than the kind of private-client stuff I do and that when – not if – it came out that their solicitor was married to the Chief of MI6, it could look like a conflict of interest and bring the firm into disrepute.'

'Why did they come to you? Not your normal sort of work.'

'No idea. Ignorance, perhaps, or if they knew maybe because they liked the idea of a little embarrassment. Anyway, you should be grateful I got out of it. Bound to be a high-profile case. Just the sort I hate.'

'The Triple A, as Whitehall now knows it, came up at the National Security Council. MI5 are worried that they're infiltrating the Scottish National Party but can't do anything about it because MI5 don't spy on British political parties.'

In fact, the AAA had not been on the agenda but had been mentioned to Charles, in what bureaucrats liked to call the margins of the meeting, by Michael Dunton, MI5's balding and genial Director General. 'Don't suppose the Triple A will cross your radar screen unless they become an international movement,' Michael said, 'but they're posing us a few problems. Not so much in themselves; they're the usual rag-bag of activists, anti-nuclear, anti-establishment, anti-capitalist, anti-everything except animal rights. We're happy to ignore them unless they're subverting parliamentary democracy or wreaking industrial havoc by violent means, in which case we're entitled to investigate them. But they pose a problem because they seem to have infiltrated the wilder shores of the SNP, the ones calling for a Scottish breakaway, a unilateral declaration of independence, and they've got several secret little things on the go which are almost certainly subversive and may be downright dangerous. But we can't investigate them without simultaneously gathering intelligence on the SNP, which is off limits, of course, and would cause enormous political ructions if it came out. So we can't do anything. Much as the government would like us to, so long as we didn't ask them first.' He smiled.

'Not a flicker on our screens,' said Charles, 'but I can ask stations to report any overseas links with like-minded groups. And they can ask their liaisons.'

'Thanks, but there's something else I wanted to ask you about.' Michael bent his head and moved a few feet away from the others, lowering his voice. 'Does the name Deep Blue mean anything? Not the chess computer but something else. Wasn't there a case, an old Sovbloc case on your side, in which it featured? I seem to remember something about it. Was it the code-name for the case? I can't be sure of anything these days. To be honest, I've not been feeling too good.'

'Your memory's better than you think. It wasn't a code-name but there was a case that featured it, the Badger case. I was the case officer. Didn't run for long. Dead case now. As is Badger himself.'

'It's just that we picked up some Internet chatter. Someone we haven't yet identified who has extremist connections was saying they – whoever "they" are – were going to get hold of Deep Blue and cause havoc. We can't work out who or what Deep Blue is, whether it's a thing or a person. I remembered it as a phrase associated with some case or other of your lot's but clearly it wasn't your agent – ex-agent – from what you say.'

'It had a colloquial meaning which I think I remember correctly but I'd need to check I've got it right.' The meeting was about to start and they were called to order. 'Let me get back to you.'

The Prime Minister wasn't chairing this time, his place taken by the Home Secretary. Alongside him was the new Foreign Secretary, Elspeth Jones, to whom, as Chief of MI6, Charles was answerable. He had had close and friendly relations with her predecessor, who had appointed him, but his meetings with Elspeth so far had been brief, formal and cautious. There was nothing to complain of but she had turned down the first submission they had put up to her, concerning Saudi Arabia, on the grounds that the political fall-out if anything went wrong was too great to be worth the risk. That was her prerogative and was the reason the submission system existed, but he sensed that it might become the pattern; she was no risk-taker, unlike her predecessor who had been unexpectedly demoted – moved sideways and brought into the innermost circle was how Downing Street spinners put it – to Chief Whip.

The meeting took its usual course, surveying threats and looming scenarios at home and abroad, with the heads of agencies and departments giving succinct opinions and the Home Secretary, unconstrained by the Prime Minister and taking advantage of Elspeth's inexperience, holding forth at length. The only unusual feature was the presence of two special political advisors, Elspeth's and the Home Secretary's. Most SPADs were not security cleared and neither of these would have been permitted to attend if the PM had chaired. By unspoken agreement, the heads of agencies and permanent secretaries all said less than they would have.

During the longueurs of the Home Secretary's peroration Charles studied the SPADs. Elspeth had introduced hers by name only – Robin Cleveley – with no explanation. Having never been in government before, she had perhaps assumed that SPADS were acceptable everywhere. Maybe they had long been political intimates, he knowing all her secrets and helping steer her to where she was, and it had not occurred to her to keep him out of anything. Her private secretary should have warned her. Charles decided he would have to mention it, if no one else did, but would start by getting his own private secretary to raise it with Elspeth's.

Cleveley, tall and tie-less, reminded him of a type he had come across first at university and later in Whitehall: confident, presentable young men with quick intelligence, rapid articulacy and the air of always being on the inside track. More attentive to superiors than inferiors, socially adroit, personally ambitious and committed to the political causes they served, they were essentially courtiers, ready, willing, anxious to please. And like courtiers of old they could, on occasion, stab.

The Home Secretary's SPAD was a woman, Melanie Stokes, short and dark-haired with sharp features and a matching quickness of manner. Charles could do nothing about her since MI6 had no locus with the

Home Office, but Michael Dunton did and would surely not approve. She intervened only once in the discussion, when the Home Secretary, looking at Michael, said that the Triple A, though sometimes posing a public order threat, should not be regarded as a security threat. It was essentially a political party operating above board and we had to be careful not to demonise it.

'Political movement,' said Melanie. 'A movement, not a party. It has no constitution. Sees itself as an expression of political will.'

The Home Secretary nodded. 'Thank you, Melanie, quite right. A movement, not a party. And not a security threat.'

The others looked for a response from Michael Dunton. As DG he had statutory authority to decide what was and was not a threat to the state, but he remained silent. Keeping his powder dry pending private discussion, Charles hoped.

After the meeting, Charles moved towards Elspeth, who was being talked at by the Home Secretary. He had no agenda with her that morning other than wanting to establish more familiar and easy relations, with more regular access. But as he edged towards her Robin Cleveley interposed himself with a broad smile and outstretched hand.

'I've never met a C before.' He used the acronym by which Chiefs of MI6 were traditionally known in Whitehall, although their names had long been public

19

knowledge. 'Robin Cleveley, the Foreign Secretary's Man Friday.'

'And much more than a Friday man, I'm sure,' said Charles, smiling in turn. It paid to be pleasant to those whose legs you wanted to cut off.

'I was wondering whether I might call on you for a chat. It seems to me, on the basis of admittedly little observation, that it might be helpful for the Secretary of State to have easier access to your views.'

It was exactly what Charles wanted, but not via Cleveley. 'Happily, if you could bear to come to Croydon.'

Robin smiled again. 'Croydon, removal therefrom, is another thing we need to talk about.'

This would have been music to Charles's ears but for the medium. He had been promised by Elspeth's predecessor that MI6 would return to Westminster, and had told his staff they would, but nothing had happened. Cleveley's initiative and his irritating assumption of equality made him feel he was being treated as another courtier, even as a supplicant. For the time being he had no option but to appear to go along with it; to show irritation in Whitehall's undeclared wars was to show weakness.

That night, with Sarah in deep sleep beside him, he listened to Big Ben striking four over the rooftops of Westminster. Perhaps she was right about eating late, though it didn't seem to affect her. He was recalling the start of the case that featured Deep Blue, decades before.

The 1980s

The Paris station, all eight of them in those days of close liaison with the French on Sovbloc and terrorist casework, were squeezed around the table in the safe speech room while Angus Copplestone, head of station, gave edited highlights of the ambassador's weekly meeting. Pale, black-haired, energetic and ambitious, an earlier version of Robin Cleveley, Angus spent as much time as he could with the ambassador. 'I must say I find myself eye to eye with him on this issue,' he would frequently say, as if announcing a surprise.

This time it was the ambassador's edict on SIS reporting on French issues – deep-chat bilaterals, Angus called it, which included anything from French positions on European Community negotiations to internal political developments and views on British policy. 'He's not keen on us reporting it, as you know, even if we do discover something the Foreign Office hasn't. It should be handled through normal Foreign Office reporting channels. I must say, I have some sympathy. It's not really secret intelligence, doesn't come from recruited agents, just officials with whom we're in liaison who say a bit more than they should. In future, therefore, anything anyone picks up should be reported to me only, orally not on paper. I'll discuss it with the ambassador and we'll decide how it should be reported to London. If it is reported – and it probably won't be – he or I will do it through Foreign Office channels. There's also no question of cultivating potential French sources or seeking intelligence on France in any form without clearance at every stage, probably all the way up to the Foreign Secretary. And it's most unlikely we'd get it. Does everyone understand that?' He looked at them all, his gaze finally settling on Charles. 'So, Charles, no more surprise weekend reports to London from your talkative French liaison partner about his government's attitudes towards the British rebate. The Foreign Office has already had Number Ten on about it, wanting more.'

'I thought the government would like to know about it, with these negotiations coming up.'

'Not your call. Above your pay grade.'

Angus's eyes stayed on Charles's for a few seconds, perhaps waiting for the acknowledging nod that was not forthcoming. For no reason Charles could define, there had been an unspoken antipathy between him and his head of station since the day he arrived. They had not argued or fallen out, there had been no overt hostility, but from the moment they shook hands he had sensed a mutual lack of sympathy, an almost intellectual estrangement. There being no issue over which they had disagreed, he had concluded it was a matter of temperament. Angus's obvious ambition and his unquestioning self-belief provoked in Charles a juvenile desire for mischievous opposition, which manifested itself as flippancy. Most of the time he hid it, but he felt that Angus picked up on it.

'The other thing,' Angus continued, returning his gaze to the others, 'is that the visiting Russian trade delegation is out of bounds. The one that's here following up last year's Paris Air Show. Charles's French liaison friends will be crawling all over them anyway so there's no need for us to get involved and risk muddying the waters. More to the point, the ambassador's pretty pally with the head of the delegation, a man called Federov, and he won't want you treading on his toes in your size twelves, Charles. Federov's a smooth operator, apparently, Party apparatchik, Central Committee fixer, blue-eyed boy of Soviet business so far as French ministers are concerned. The ambassador's trying to get his delegation invited to London on the back of this visit, so a big Keep off the Grass sign, OK?'

The meeting moved on to everyone's plans for the week ahead. At the end Angus asked Charles to stay behind. 'Not many morsels on your plate at the moment, I know,' he said as the steel door closed on the others. 'Not your fault, of course, that we're unable to do everything we want but with this secondee from MI5 coming out to take over all your IRA stuff with French liaison you'll have even fewer toys to play with. And as everyone else's plates are pretty full I'm afraid I'm going to have to ask you to take on a little chore.'

He smiled as he pushed a paper with a list of agent

numbers across the table. His smile, like his regret-ful tone, always seemed too deliberate. None of the numbers meant anything to Charles except that they signified individuals rather than subjects.

'Pensioners,' Angus continued, 'former agents of various nationalities living in France to whom the Office pays pensions for one reason or another. Some of them go back to the Second World War and we have to check annually that they're still alive. You might find you can cross a couple off. They drop off their perches every year.' He smiled at the thought. 'Interesting reading for anyone with time for that sort of thing. Normally I get one of the secretaries to do it but they've all got more important things to do at the moment. You don't have to do much. Just look them up over a cup of tea or coffee or glass of whatever stronger stuff is keeping them going.'

The files were mostly single volumes, beginning with summaries culled from multi-volume files held in Head Office of the agents' services before they retired to France. They also comprised records of visits, pension payments, illnesses, requests and, in one or two cases, deaths of spouses. Others, whose connections with British officialdom were no secret, contained copies of invitations to the embassy's annual Queen's Birthday garden party.

Charles spent the rest of the day in the station, leafing through them. He hated days spent at his desk without getting out and about, though his colleagues seemed not to mind. Officers on most stations were generally out meeting people, which was how they got their business, or doing their Foreign Office cover jobs partly with that aim in mind. But Angus equated work with physical presence and liked to see his officers at their desks, reading and writing; out of sight meant out of control. But out of sight was where Charles intended to be, once he had decided his order of visits. Two were pleasingly distant, one near the Swiss border, another in Cherbourg. The others were in and around Paris but he reckoned he could stretch them to several days, allowing half a day each.

His first was to an elderly French couple who lived in the rue d'Astorg, not far from the Arc de Triomphe and near a corner café he sometimes used. He lunched there and called on them afterwards. They had served both SIS and SOE (Special Operations Executive) during the war and had been betrayed while working for the latter. They had survived torture and imprisonment but had been ignored by de Gaulle and successive French governments because they had worked for the British. SIS had paid them a small pension ever since their liberation.

Their small apartment was crowded with ornaments and knick-knacks. Charles had the impression of quiet, forgotten lives and of absolute dependency on each other. They seemed as grateful for the brief annual contact, with the bottle and flowers he had brought, as for their pension. It reminded them they had been part of something, they said. Also that, 'London never forgets'. It took little prompting to get them to talk about their own operational pasts. Charles much preferred hearing about the war and early Cold War to processing paper back in the station. But they did not talk about their torture and imprisonment.

His next visit was to Machemont, a small town an hour or so outside Paris. It was not clear from the file why Josef, the elderly Russian émigré, was paid a pension. The summary showed that he had been imprisoned in Russia but not for working for SIS; he had been recruited only after leaving. Since then he had performed various services, mostly introductions to or personality reports on visiting Russian officials whom he cultivated as a sympathetic freelance journalist. His intelligence stream, always modest, had petered out over the years as his access dwindled. He had been paid more generously than the results merited and the file recorded his award of a pension without indicating why. It was likely that successive case officers had liked him and had found it more congenial to be nice than to acknowledge declining productivity. His French wife seemed wealthy in her own right. The most recent paper was a letter from Head Office pointing out that, although a pensioner, he was still classified as an agent and that he saw himself as continuing to work for the Office, regarding his pension as a salary. There was no indication that he was in need of money and no prospect of his regaining any useful access; he should therefore be terminated, politely and considerately, with – if the station thought necessary – a year's pension as a terminal bonus.

Angus had written on the letter: *Clearly one of the Old Scroungers Brigade. Terminate without bonus if poss but <u>do terminate</u>*. That was how Charles met Josef, and how the Badger case started.

Chapter Three

The 1980s

'Another glass, Mr Thoroughgood. Or a little cognac?'

'Thank you, Josef, but, no, really, I'm driving. Anyway, it's Charles, please.'

'Yvette, some coffee for Mr Thoroughgood.'

'It's Charles, please call me Charles.'

Josef shook his head. 'To me you are Mr Thoroughgood. It is a sign of respect. Not for you personally – though I do respect you, even after one lunch – but for the Service. Yvette can call you Charles and you must call me Josef but I insist on respecting the Service that helped me in difficult times when I was first here and which fights the war we fight together. My first case officer, Major Mackenzie, he taught me that the Service always keeps its word. You did not know him, you are absurdly young. Everyone is.'

He raised his glass again, his bright dark eyes almost disappearing in his round wrinkled face. He had bushy grey eyebrows and thick iron-grey hair. Everything about him was thick: his stubby fingers, his wide head, his shoulders, neck and thighs, which stretched his trousers. He looked as if he had been compressed and compacted by enormous forces and now could be compressed no more, like a dense, irreducible rock. But a jovial and vigorous rock.

Yvette, diminutive and almost silent, left them. They were lunching on the terrace overlooking a hay meadow at the back of the attractive and modest chateau outside Marchemont. It had been occupied by German troops during the Second World War and Allied shelling had knocked it about, destroying both wings. 'It is my contribution to the Great Patriotic War,' Josef had said, 'to occupy the fascist headquarters.'

He held his glass and looked at Charles. 'Are you another fly-by-night or are you my new case officer? I regard myself as still in arms, you know, still working, though it is seldom anyone comes to debrief me and most of the time I have nothing to report anyway.'

He spoke in mixed French and English, the latter heavily accented, cultivated and archaic, a voice from another world. Charles liked listening to it, but didn't like what he himself had to say next. 'I'm not your new case officer, I'm afraid.'

'Another fly-by-night, then? You visit to see if I am alive, to check you are not paying a corpse?'

'I'm supposed to terminate you.'

Josef's eyes were submerged again by wrinkled flesh.

'Sir, you must please understand that in my world that word had a meaning different to that which I presume you intend.'

Charles smiled back. 'And in my world it means even less than you think. It means that I record that you have been told that you are no longer regarded as an active agent and that you are to be thanked for your service by—'

'You are children.' Josef ceased smiling as he leaned forward and helped himself to a Montecristo cigar from the box on the table. He offered the packet to Charles, who didn't want another but felt he should accept. He had followed his host in using empty plates as ashtrays.

'By which I mean you are not serious.' Josef paused as they both lit from his lighter. 'You think spying is a job. But in this world – our world – it is a crusade. An old spy does not cease to be a spy when he loses access. He is still a soldier – he still has his gun – even when he is not in the front line. He can still help in an encounter with the enemy. You should never tell him he is no longer any use. You should simply say, "Here is how to contact us. We do not forget you. Ring us if you find anything interesting." It will not happen often, sometimes he will waste your time, but sometimes it happens.'

'Of course, yes, that's really what—'

'You have not suffered, that is your trouble. For you the Cold War is like a football match, like your English football league, some games you win and some you lose and then you go home. You do not understand what it is to live under communism. It is not a game and you can't go home. You must learn that, Mr Thoroughgood.'

Josef's face had reddened and his dark eyes glistened. Charles's reaction to any display of emotion was to seek to ameliorate it. 'I agree, Josef, we have not suffered but we do understand it is a war, a war of beliefs and values, a war of ideas. Probably our manner, the manners of people like me, make us seem—'

'Casual and complacent. If you seem, you are. Major Mackenzie was not. He wouldn't have survived if he had been. He had fought Nazism, he understood communism, he recognised realities, he knew what these systems, these people, are like.'

'So do we, do I – I hope. I know that they believe—'

'No.' Josef raised his voice and waved his cigar. 'They believe in nothing. That is what you in the West do not understand. They say to you and to each other in public, they say Marx, they say Lenin, they justify themselves. But it's clothes, that's all, they clothe themselves in it, like a religion. But really it's power, keeping power, that's all they want. They don't care about the people, they are not interested in ideas, they just want to keep hold of power. The whole system, the whole country, is corrupt, completely. They all know it and they all pretend it isn't. Russia is for sale, I promise you. You could buy it if you understood it. There are no real communists in Russia, they are all in the West, in your universities, in your newspapers, your BBC. Have you noticed what happens to those who go to live in Russia or other communist countries? They never get on, they are never happy. Because they are communist, they are really communist when they arrive, but no one else is. Certainly no one in the Communist Party of the Soviet Union. They are for the Communist Party, not communism.'

Yvette arrived with coffees and biscuits on an elaborately painted tray. Josef's smile reappeared. 'My dear, I am trying to educate Mr Thoroughgood. He thinks members of the CPSU are communists.'

Yvette smiled at Charles. 'Josef has strong beliefs. You must think for yourself.'

Afterwards, Josef walked Charles to his car on the drive at the front of the house. He took Charles's arm. 'So I am being terminated, you call it? This is our first and last meeting. After my many years of work?'

Charles felt awkward and reluctant but his instructions were clear. Josef had had nothing to report for years. 'I'm afraid—'

'A sadness for me but a tragedy for MI6. And the tragedy is, you don't know why.'

Charles stopped, his hand on his car door. 'Tell me why.'

'Because you don't understand how rotten your enemy is, rotten inside. Mrs Thatcher and President Reagan, they worry about Soviet nuclear missiles, SS-20s. But you don't understand, if you want to know more about SS-20s you can have one, you buy one. I am serious. If you offer the crew a home in the West they will drive it across the border for you, through the Iron Curtain. You can have it.'

Charles had heard this sort of thing before. Perhaps it was true but the practicalities seemed insuperable. And it always came down to practicalities. He held out his hand. 'You may be right, Josef, and if you ever work out how we can speak to an SS-20 crew, let me know. You have the number.'

Josef ignored his hand. 'I tell you now. The man who can do it is here, underneath your nose. Igor Federov. I can introduce you.'

'You know him?'

'From the camp.'

'He was in the camp? Then how did he—'

'How did he climb up this greasy pole all the way to the Central Committee? He is clever man and he betray everyone, that's how.' Josef took Charles's arm again and began walking him towards the lawn, away from his car. 'In the camps you learn the truth about the system that sent you there. You must understand this thing. This system, it stink like shit, it taste like shit, it is shit. You know it because you are inside the communist arse. They have made you into shit. If they let you out you can do three things. Keep quiet and hope no one ever notices you again, which is what most people do. Or you get out, right out, you escape the system like I did. Very few can do this, I was lucky.

Or you take your revenge by climbing back up the greasy pole and make the system serve you. Even fewer people do that but Igor did. That is what he has done. He is there for himself, only himself, and if he thinks you can help him, he will help you. And if he thinks you are in his way, you are back down the pole, in the shit. Whoosh!' Josef sliced the air with his free hand.

'You still know him? Will you see him while he's here?'

'If I contact him he will see me. It was a camp friendship. Such things are not forgotten.'

'Could you persuade him to meet us – me?'

'If you have something he wants. I can ask.'

Charles unhooked Josef from his arm and shook hands again. 'Termination suspended.'

Josef's moist dark eyes disappeared again. 'You are learning, Mr Thoroughgood. One day you will be Major Mackenzie.'

Chapter Four

The Present

Charles's desire to indulge his irritation did not quite overcome his wisdom in hiding it, but it was a close-run thing. It was the day following the NSC meeting and Robin Cleveley was sitting in Charles's office with a cup of coffee, looking about him as if they were sharing a private joke.

'I knew Croydon was – well, not where you want to be, but I'd no idea it was ... I mean, this building, it's so awful it's worth preserving. Preferably with the remains of the architect on display in the entrance, crumbling with his creation.' Robin laughed.

Charles forced a smile. The appointment had taken him by surprise. It was in his calendar, as his private secretary pointed out. He disliked his screen calendar because entries could appear and disappear without his knowledge whereas with his pocket diary he had physically to enter or delete. He would not have agreed an appointment with Robin Cleveley if he had known.

'I do put all new entries in red,' Elaine had said, no doubt hiding her own irritation. 'But you do have to look at it now and again.'

Charles held up his hands. 'Mea culpa, mea maxima culpa.'

'It's a bit late to cancel now.'

Charles nodded.

What made it more irritating was that Robin had come to discuss moving MI6 back into central London, speaking with the authority of the Foreign Secretary. 'Elspeth wants you there, very much so, and she's tasked me with sorting it. We've looked at a number of options, including squeezing you back into a couple of floors in the old MI6 headquarters at Vauxhall Cross. But I thought perhaps you wouldn't want to share it with a hotel. Hope that was right? Best option by far, cheapest, soon to be available and most central, is a return to that building at the bottom of Victoria Street where you went after Vauxhall Cross. Of course, you'd have to share it with the DTs – Department for Trade – and some PR companies and you'd only get two floors, but they are the top ones and you're smaller than you were. But there's a fly in the ointment. D'you know Melanie Stokes? Home Secretary's head SPAD, my equivalent. She was at the meeting the other day. They – she – want it for their beefed-up immigration unit. You know, the one that lets the wrong ones in, keeps the right ones out. Lot of political pressure. Melanie's determined and poisonous and she's got a head start.'

SPADS always seemed to love or loathe each other, more often loathing those from the same political tribe. 'D'you mean they have first option, or what?'

'I mean, she heard that we were considering it for you and so realised it was available. She's trying to get the Home Sec to take it to cabinet and veto it on the grounds that it sends a signal that the government is encouraging spying and that you're a controversial appointment. Because of your history, that is. Nothing personal. Nothing personal at all.'

'Elspeth's predecessor promised we'd be back in Whitehall. Gave me his word.'

'But then he got moved. We're serious about it, I promise you. We want you back.'

They kicked the subject around but got no further. It was left that Robin would get the Foreign Secretary to mention it informally to the Prime Minister and then Robin would press ahead. Charles had to swallow his dislike of dealing with courtiers, and keep it down.

'One other thing.' Robin paused at the door. 'Does the name Deep Blue mean anything?'

'Chess computer. Why?'

'That's what I thought.' He looked as if he were about to add something, then changed his mind. 'Thanks. Goodbye.'

Charles stayed late again that evening going through the Badger file. It had sat in his security cupboard all day like an alcoholic's secret supply, the thought of it a sly comfort in the interstices of meetings, emails and questions about his proposal that all important or costly operations should be subjected to impact assessments. It was not only Robin Cleveley's question that kept reminding him of Badger but his earlier iteration of 'nothing personal'. Angus Copplestone had used the identical phrasing decades before in Paris, when sacking him.

The 1980s

'You must understand, Charles, that it's nothing personal, nothing personal at all. It's just that the MI5 officer we're getting will take over a substantial slice of your liaison job – it would hardly be fair to give him less, since that's why he's being posted here – and Head Office in their wisdom have decided that your talents would best be deployed back in London.'

'I shall be very sorry to go.'

'I shall be very sorry to lose you.' They smiled in mutual insincerity. 'I'm sure Personnel will find you a decent perch in London. You're not due your annual confidential report yet but I'll do an interim end-of-post one. Unfortunately, I won't be able to avoid mentioning your recent refusal to terminate that useless old agent. Your suggestion that we could use an old has-been like him to get alongside a Central Committee operator like Federov was frankly naïve. Politically naïve, too. I thought I'd made it clear that the ambassador and the Foreign Office wouldn't let us within a million miles of Federov. But I hope that won't count too much against you. You don't seem to have dropped any balls with liaison, which was your main thing, of course.'

Charles nodded. If he argued Angus would simply add that he couldn't take criticism. 'Thanks.'

'Thank you, Charles. The station will miss you.'

Back in London, Charles had been made assistant desk officer to the European Community Liaison Team. He shared an office with Mike, a man a few years older whom he assumed must have done something wrong to be posted there. It was soon apparent, however, that Mike, so far from doing anything wrong, never did anything at all. He introduced Charles to office climbing, in which the aim was to get all round the perimeter walls of the office without touching the floor. It was a ritual for newcomers to the section and the record was held by the legendary Freddie Farquarson, who had gone off the rails in Rio.

'What did he do?'

'Four minutes thirty-two. Like a bloody monkey.'

'In Rio, I mean.'

'All got hushed up but if it's Rio it's sex. Foreign Office has a history of heads of mission going off the rails there. Last but one just went AWOL. Never seen again until our head of station ran into him in a brothel. He was the barman. You need to get both feet on the ledge or you won't get across to the next window. Holding the blinds not allowed.'

41

Charles was spread-eagled between a security cabinet and the window ledge. They were on the fourteenth floor of Century House, with a panoramic view of Lambeth and south London. The door opened and Harold, their boss, entered. Tall, bald and bespectacled, he was nearing retirement and looked permanently, wearily, puzzled. 'When you've a moment, Charles.' He pulled the door to.

Charles jumped down. 'My usual good timing.'

'Don't worry, nothing surprises Harold. Anyway, he knows all about office climbing. Reckons in this section we need something to keep us awake. Apparently after the war when Head Office was in Broadway Buildings they used to chuck thunder-flashes under people's desks when they nodded off. More a military culture then, I guess. Everything was.'

Harold's desk faced his office window so that his back was to the door. He did not look up until Charles stood beside him. His puzzled expression deepened before clearing. 'Ah, Charles, yes, thanks for dropping by. C/Sovbloc – Hookey – wants to see you. Gather he knows you. You've worked for him before.'

'I was involved with one of his operations.'

'Well, you'd better cut along and see him. Shouldn't say anything to Mike if this is going to be hush-hush Sovbloc secret squirrel business.'

'Sorry about – when you came in just now, I was just ...'

Harold shook his head. 'Anything to relieve Head

Office tedium. I'd be more inclined to jump out of the window than straddle it if I were your age. I'm stuck here till I go, of course, but with luck a better berth will come along for you. Maybe Hookey's got something up his sleeve. Good man, Hookey. Got character. Not much of that about in the Office these days. Used to be, of course. Used to be some wonderful characters around.' He gazed through the window as if at a parade of wonderful old Office characters. He seemed to have forgotten Charles.

'I'll go and see him, then.'

'What?' Harold looked round. 'Yes, good idea, yes.' When Charles reached the door he spoke again. 'Don't suppose you've had a chance to do that paper on European threat-warning restructuring strategy yet?'

'Mike and I were talking about it the other day.'

'No need to rush it. No one will notice if we don't contribute at all. MI5 are bound to send reams of stuff, anyway. But if we do send something there'll be a conference jolly for you or Mike in Rome or Stockholm or somewhere.'

'We'll get on with it, then.'

'Nothing too long, mind. Unless you don't want anyone to read it.'

C/Sovbloc's empire was on the twelfth floor, a quiet floor because, unlike all the others, the office doors were closed. Hookey occupied the corner overlooking Waterloo station, protected by his secretary's outer office. She was Maureen, a tweedy, kindly-looking woman in her forties whom Charles knew from earlier involvement in another Sovbloc case.

'Charles, this is a nice surprise, how are you?' She smiled as she discreetly covered the papers in her in-tray with an empty file folder. She had no pending tray and the out-tray was already covered. 'I knew his lordship was looking for you. I'll just see if he's disturbable.' As in the Foreign Office, there was a convention that no one knocked on doors. She stood in the doorway so that Charles couldn't see. Hookey murmured something, papers were shuffled and a security cabinet closed. Maureen stood aside and smiled.

Hookey was a short man wearing glasses and a grey cardigan, with his suit jacket hung over the back of his controller's large swivel chair. He had a pale, thoughtful face and grey eyes which gave nothing away.

'Happy to be back from Paris?'

'In some ways.'

'One of which must be the absence from your life of Angus Copplestone. Not a marriage made in heaven. Doubtless he feels the same. Where are you now?'

Charles told him.

'Best thing you can do there is sabotage the wretched EC. If only we were allowed to penetrate it. Anyway, I've got something else for you. Not another job, I'm afraid, but a minor and I hope not too bothersome distraction. You're still in your flat in the Boltons?'

'Just moved back in. Luckily, the tenant—'

'Good. MI5 want to use it.' He explained that MI5 were interested in the couple who had moved into the flat below Charles's, middle-aged Canadians who ran a rare book and map business from home. 'Or so they purport to be. MI5 suspect they may be Russian illegals, intelligence officers deployed under natural cover in the West to handle cases too sensitive or too awkward for the KGB residency in the embassy. Remember the Krogers, Lonsdale and the Portland dockyard spy ring and all that? Same sort of thing, only MI5 have got no idea what they're up to or even whether they're definitely illegals.

'Anyway, they've obviously got enough on them to justify a warrant for a tech-op. Probe mikes, I guess. They did the usual neighbour checks and were delighted to find you lived upstairs. Assuming, that is, that you're willing to act as listening post and have part of your flat cluttered with their gear and your floorboards drilled through and all that?'

'Yes, of course, I—'

'No money in it, of course, as you're one of us. You might get the odd bottle of plonk. They're keen, they want to get on with it, so you'd better go over today. Provided the arduous duties of your new section will permit your temporary absence. Maureen will tell you who to see over there. Any questions?'

Hookey never had time for small talk or gossip. Charles's hand was on the door handle when he decided to take a chance. 'Do you mind if I briefly mention the immediate cause of my leaving Paris? One of them, anyway.'

'So long as you're not asking for my opinion of that unctuous creep Copplestone.'

'It's about a man called Federov, head of the Soviet trade delegation to the Paris Air Show, and a former Russian access agent whom I was supposed to terminate but didn't. They were in a prison camp together and the access agent—'

'Come back and sit down.'

The story shrank in the telling. There was really very little to it and he realised as he spoke that what had swayed him was the intensity of Josef's conviction that Federov was biddable and the Soviet system rotten to the core. He could convey nothing of that intensity and felt it would not impress Hookey anyway, who had doubtless heard it all before.

But Hookey listened, slouched back in his chair, his hands pushed into his cardigan pockets. When Charles finished he leaned forward and made a note on the single piece of paper on his desk. 'How long is the trade delegation there for?'

'I'm not sure. It was still there last week.'

'Is anyone else seeing this access agent?'

'Doubt it. Unless Angus has sent someone to terminate him.'

The three phones on Hookey's desk were coloured red, black and grey. He picked up the grey one. 'Maureen, could you find out from the French A

46

section whether the Russian trade delegation is still in Paris and when it's due to leave. Also, get the file of a Paris access agent number – number, Charles?' He put the phone down. 'Bugger off to MI5 now and then come back and see me before close of play tonight. Does anyone else know about this?'

'Only Angus, though I imagine others in the Paris station will have got to know about it.'

'Keep it that way.'

The MI5 building was an anonymous grey office block at the top of Gower Street. Technical operations were planned by A branch, where Charles was thanked for his help and told to regard himself as part of the team.

'We won't make too much of a mess of your flat,' said a portly man called Steve. 'Anything we do we make good, better than it was. We've got these new silent drills which they'll never hear, especially as we'll only drill when they're out.' He laughed and handed Charles a mug of coffee. 'We've been through plans of the building but it would be helpful now if you could indicate which rooms you use for what and what's in them. We'll need to sort out somewhere to hide the recording kit, somewhere out of your way and not visible to visitors. You live alone, don't you?'

'Yes, but I have a girlfriend who stays sometimes.'

'She in the Office or conscious?'

'Neither.' Janet worked in the HR department of a major chain store. Charles had never made her aware of the real nature of his work, maintaining the fiction of his Foreign Office cover.

'That could be a problem.'

'There's quite a bit of space and an empty cupboard in the spare bedroom. I could bring some of my junk from my mother's house to hide things.'

They were joined by a tall woman in her thirties with startling red hair that looked as if it had been electrocuted. She was the Russian Illegals section desk officer. 'Sue, Sue North. Have you met them, the Turnips?' she asked as they shook hands. 'Don't worry, that's just the name we've given them because they're both dumpy and round. Known to the world as Stephen and Diane Melbury, in their forties, dealers in rare books, manuscripts and maps. Moved here from Toronto three months ago. We reckon they must keep all their stuff in the flat because there's no indication of a storage place elsewhere and they get a lot of business mail, parcels of books and so on. Whether that's enough to make a plausible living, we can't say. Doubtful, I think.'

'Why are you interested in them?'

'Canadian liaison put us on to them when they left Canada. The original lead came from the Americans but I can't say any more about that. The Canadians checked out their histories and all seemed OK at first but then someone noticed that both birth certificates are identical to babies born in Toronto who died within a year or two of each other. The FBI have also been on to us about them. So, you've not met them? Or seen them on the stairs? Or ever been in their flat?' She had strong dark eyebrows which she raised with each question.

'No, but I could easily contrive a reason to call. Introduce myself in a neighbourly way.'

'That would be helpful, wouldn't it?' Her eyebrows went up again as she looked at Steve and his two colleagues. 'Ideally, they'd invite you in for a drink so you could get an idea of what's where in the flat and the best places for mikes, that sort of thing. But only if it's easy and natural. Last thing we want is to arouse suspicions.'

He couldn't easily place her accent, partly because it seemed to come and go. He guessed Midlands, somewhere.

'All we need now is a date to recce your place,' said Steve. 'Best when they're not there but according to telecheck they're not often out together. Boring life, whatever it is. Could a couple of us come round as friends of yours for a drink one evening?'

'I'll show you out,' said Sue.

It was after six when Charles returned to Century House, by which time most sections had closed for the night. Maureen was still at her desk and Hookey at his, working in a subdued pool of light thrown by his green-shaded table lamp, the strip-lights turned off. It was such memories of Hookey that, years later, prompted Charles to get his own lamp. Hookey was smoking his pipe and reading a file, which he covered as Charles entered.

'Have you made them happy bunnies in Gower Street?'

'I think so. They—'

'Our friend Federov is still in Paris. He's due to come on here, as you know, but it's obviously more natural for your chap to make contact with him there. Trouble is, we've only got two days to do it. Can you ring your chap, fly to Paris tonight or at sparrow's fart in the morning and brief him on what to say to Federov if he can get to him? His number's in his Head Office file, which is with Maureen.'

'Yes, but what about the Paris station? If they—'

Hookey waved his pipe. 'Copplestone must know nothing of our interest in Federov. He'd go bleating to his ambassador, who'd get the Foreign Office to put the kybosh on it. We might be able to argue the case but it would take days and we'd miss him. Go and ring now and then come back and have a whisky. We need to agree what your chap should say to him. And what you'll say if you get to him.'

Chapter Five

The Present

Michael Dunton, Director General of MI5, had a heart attack on the day he and Charles were due to lunch. He had been feeling unwell the week before, his office said, but had come into work that day saying he felt better. Then, during a meeting with his directors, he was stricken by pains in his chest and arms. He was taken across the river to St Thomas's, where he was found to be in the midst of an attack. He was alive and would undergo surgery but the prognosis was not yet clear. His wife was at the hospital. The DDG – Deputy Director General, Simon Mall – would take over for the time being. Was there anything Charles needed to discuss urgently?

There wasn't. It was their routine monthly catch-up at which they resolved issues, usually turf disputes, that their respective staffs had failed to sort out at lower levels. They also agreed joint tactics on wider Whitehall issues. He could have done it all with Simon

Mall but found his company depressing to the point of lowering the room temperature. A grey man in every sense, albeit honest and conscientious and not at all dislikeable, he exemplified the precautionary principle to a degree that – as Michael Dunton himself had once disloyally remarked – would have prevented evolution. Charles proposed that the meeting should wait until Michael's fate became clearer.

He felt vindicated when Elaine, his private secretary, came in to say that she'd just heard something from MI5 private office.

'What's happened to him?'

'Not about the DG, or not directly. No, they told the Home Office that the DDG would take over for the time being. Then ten minutes later the Home Secretary himself rang the DDG to say that although he could continue to run the service in Michael Dunton's absence he – the Home Secretary – wanted to send his SPAD over in a supervisory role. That's the dreaded Melanie Stokes everyone talks about.'

'What does he mean by "supervisory role"? Who's actually running it, her or Simon?'

'They don't know. They're all in a tizz about it. The Home Secretary mentioned "overseeing intra-Whitehall relations" but no one knows what that means.'

'Poor old Simon. He may not be God's gift but he doesn't deserve that. What do you know about Melanie Stokes?'

'Only that she's a prize ...' Elaine smiled. 'D'you want me to spell it out?'

'Robin Cleveley thinks the same. That might have made me think well of her except that she's trying to stop us moving back to Whitehall. Find out what you can – basic biog details – and let me know.'

'Know thine enemy?'

'Plus any gossip.'

Elaine had been a private secretary in the Foreign Office before moving to work for Charles and was well known in the Whitehall private secretarial network. Private office staff were efficient and their cooperation with each other went beyond formal inter-departmental relations. She reappeared later that day, notebook in hand. 'Melanie Stokes. Shall I close the door?'

She sat, smiling. 'Quite a girl. Born in Bermuda to a Spanish mother and British father who was later imprisoned for embezzlement and seems to have faded from the scene. Got to Oxford, got a first in Modern Languages, ran off with her tutor pursued by vengeful wife, dumped him, went through two think-tanks in quick succession – in every sense, I gather – and got to know the Home Sec socially – at least, that was the word used – when he was shadow spokesman. Then got taken on as his SPAD and the rest we know. Has a live-in partner, an older man who – wait for it – is a Triple A activist. Said to run a secret group they don't admit to called Direct Action. He does a lot of social media and occasional press pieces for left-of-centre publications. Occasionally seen at demos but doesn't show his face very often. No suggestion that she is influenced by his views but no one who knows them can understand what they're doing together. She fights the Home Office corner aggressively, as you may have noticed. Whatever the argument.'

'Do we have a name for the partner?'

'Micklethwaite.' She leafed through her notebook. 'Can't remember his first name, not sure I—'

'James. James Anthony, known to friends and family as Jam. Or used to be.'

'You know him?'

'Knew. I used to go out with his sister, about a hundred years ago, in the Eighties. There was no Triple A then but he was involved with CND and the Greenham Common nuclear protest. He has quite a past, too.'

'Sounds as if he's not alone.'

Charles smiled. 'Mine's nothing like as colourful, I'm afraid.' As she left he added, 'Couldn't do me another favour, could you? Find out whether there's a lady in MI5 called Sue North. She'd be a certain age, like me. Probably left years ago.'

The rest of the afternoon was taken up with his finance people, rehearsing forthcoming budget negotiations with the Treasury. Elsewhere in the building, he couldn't help reflecting, other people were planning operations, recounting those they'd been on, assessing and issuing reports, discussing this agent's motivation or that one's future, drafting recruitment proposals. Or room climbing, for all he knew – though open-plan offices had presumably put a stop to a lot of that sort of thing. Quite possibly to other forms of fun, too. There didn't seem to be so much laughter these days, or jokes, particularly practical jokes. Perhaps it was his age, perhaps Elaine's generation were having a rollicking good time which they suppressed in his presence. He hoped so. Laughter and jokes were good for any organisation. Irresponsible sometimes, time-wasting maybe, but good for morale. He would ask her. He wouldn't bother asking his board of directors, whom he doubted could spell 'fun'.

The budget meeting ended late on a predictably cheerless note. He would talk to the heads of the other agencies, with whom he both competed and cooperated over the single Intelligence vote. But who did that mean in MI5 now? Simon Mall would have complete command of all the details but it was hard to imagine him standing up to the Treasury. Had Melanie Stokes been sent to clip MI5's wings or would she become its doughty defender against cuts?

Elaine was still at her desk in his outer office, seeing it as part of her job to be there when he arrived and when he left unless he sent her home. She tore off a sheet from her pad and held it up. 'The lady you were asking about, Sue North. She's still there, runs their vetting section. This is her number.'

'You should go home, there's nothing else for tonight.'

'You're tucking up in bed with your old files again?'

'Only an hour or so. Or two.'

Chapter Six

The 1980s

'But he wouldn't come here. He couldn't. You put him in danger just by asking.' Charles had said it to Josef three times now and wondered whether he was being too patient. 'Look, Federov has a very busy schedule, he's flying to London the day after tomorrow, it would take half a day to come here to Marchemont, see you and get back. He'd have to explain his absence to his delegation, which is bound to include a KGB minder, and even if he feels secure enough to be honest and say he's seeing his old friend, he's taking a big risk. Something that would be used against him by enemies on the Central Committee and elsewhere. And he has enemies, we know that. And he's very cautious, which is how he's survived. He won't come, he can't. You'll have to go to him.'

They were in Josef's kitchen, a high-tiled room, spotlessly clean. Yvette had made coffee and was sitting silently at the end of the table.

Josef raised his hands in a gesture of theatrical helplessness. 'How can I go to him? I am not a pilot or an aircraft maker. Where would we meet? I cannot stay in the George the Fifth, the most expensive hotel in Paris. No. I must ring him and say, "Oleg, it is I, Josef. Come and see me." He will come, I promise, Mr Thoroughgood.'

'He won't, he can't. He lives in a goldfish bowl. The only way to see him is for you to jump in with him.'

Josef looked comically serious and spoke in lowered tones. 'Mr Thoroughgood, forgive me, please. You were not in the camp with us. When he hears my voice, he will come. You will be here and I will introduce you and he will spy for you. You see. I will ring now.' He stood.

Charles stood. He hoped Yvette wouldn't laugh, because if she did he knew he would. 'If you do, I'll go.' Neither moved until Charles sat again. 'Sit down, please. I have a plan.' He waited while Josef slowly sat. Yvette stared at her husband. There was silence. Charles continued quietly, hoping that Josef's need for theatre was satisfied. 'You will ring the George the Fifth and book yourselves in for tonight and tomorrow night, both of you. You will wait in the bar or restaurant or reception until Oleg Federov comes in and, ideally, sees you. If he doesn't see you, you approach him.'

'You will pay?'

'Of course.'

'For us both?'

Charles nodded. Hookey had not mentioned a budget but it was too late to worry now. 'You try to get some time alone with him over coffee or a drink, in his room or wherever, and you—'

'I tell him about you. I say you will meet him.'

'You don't mention me. You talk about him. You find out whether there is anything he wants that we can do for him. You offer help and you try to establish a discreet means of contact. If he's not alone, or if he seems awkward, you don't push it, you simply be nice and—'

'If we do not meet you will still—'

'We will still pay. Everything. Have a nice time there. Look upon it as a bonus to your pension.'

There was a pause. 'I have never been to the George the Fifth,' said Yvette.

The next evening, Charles strode into the hotel with an attempt at confident familiarity, looking neither to his right nor left. He knew Josef's room number and didn't want to draw attention to him by asking reception. Had he looked about he would have noticed the gathering of people to the right and the taped-off area to the left, attended by police and security guards. One of the latter stretched out his arm and shepherded Charles into the taped area, which contained a small crush of resentful hotel guests. Important visitors, somehow identified to the police, wandered unhindered to the throng on the right. Every so often, after checking by the security guards, one of his fellow captives was released to the rest of the hotel. As he queued for his pre-release interrogation, resigned to having to give Josef's name after all, he gathered that the party was for VIPs from the air show. More of them arrived.

'What are you doing here?' At first there was more puzzlement than affront in Angus Copplestone's face.

'Visiting my girlfriend.' It was an impromptu cover. He should have thought before. Always have an explanation for wherever you are or whoever you're with, his trainers used to say, again and again.

'Some girlfriend, if she's staying here.'

'International lawyer. The clients pay.'

Angus half-turned as the party he was with veered towards the throng on the right. His movement caught the ambassador's eye as he was enumerating to a man Charles assumed to be Federov the advantages of buying Rolls-Royce aero engines for civil airlines. Federov, who had tired dark eyes and greying black hair, looked bored and indifferent. The ambassador was distracted. 'Charles, I thought you'd gone back.'

'He's on private business, sir,' said Angus.

'Really?' The ambassador looked sceptical. The whole party stopped. Apart from the Russians there was the head of chancery, the commercial counsellor and members of the British trade delegation. The guard, assuming that Charles should have been part of the party, lifted the tape for him. Charles felt obliged to go through and found himself alongside Federov who, mistaking him for someone important, held out his hand.

'I am Igor Federov.' His English was slow and heavily accented.

'Charles Thoroughgood.'

'Formerly second secretary at the embassy here,' said Angus anxiously. 'Back in London now. He's here on private business.' The party moved on as he spoke. He followed without a backward glance at Charles.

Yvette was flushed and smiling when she opened the door, in Russian fashion standing back to let Charles cross the threshold before shaking hands. The room was palatial, with heavy, richly coloured curtains and drapes and a profusion of armchairs, sofas and flowers. It was suffocatingly warm and smelled of alcohol and coffee. Bottles and clothes were strewn about as after a party. It had not occurred to Charles that they would take a suite.

'Josef sleeps,' said Yvette.

'I'm sorry, I'll come back later. Do you know if he—'

'This room is beautiful. Would you like vodka?'

'No, thank you, I'll just—'

'I understand. You want champagne.' She giggled as she poured some into the nearest glass, which was used. Her hand was unsteady.

'Mr Thoroughgood!' Josef was out of sight, in the bedroom, his voice a throaty roar.

'Josef wakes,' said Yvette.

'I come, I come!' roared Josef. 'You are beautiful man, Mr Thoroughgood. MI6 is beautiful man. All are beautiful men. We have beautiful day. Wait. I come.'

In the minute or so before he emerged, Yvette pottered unsteadily about the room, muttering to herself in several languages. She put two red roses in a half-full champagne bottle and placed it carefully in the middle of the sofa. Josef appeared, walking towards Charles as if aboard ship in a head wind and long cross-swell. He was clad in a white bathrobe and smoking the stub of a cigar. His embrace was a concoction of alcohol, tobacco and after-shave.

'Have you spoken to Federov?' Charles asked, on release.

Josef sat suddenly on the sofa, upsetting the champagne, which he ignored and Yvette didn't notice. 'You ask if I speak to Federov? Yvette, he ask if I speak to Oleg.'

Yvette paused, holding another bottle and more flowers. 'You must tell him.'

Josef looked at Charles with outspread arms and raised eyebrows. 'My oldest friend, my friend of the camps? Do I speak to him?'

'Have you?'

'How can he not speak to Josef, his oldest friend, his friend of the camps?'

It had become clear to Charles that his role in Josef's theatre was always to be the straight man. He should show neither impatience nor mockery, but it was hard not to smile. 'Have you spoken to him?'

'He is important man, he is *nomenklatura*, he *has people* around him all the time, they are with him, they watch him, he knows state secrets. The French, they want to do deals with him, your British ambassador, he follows him like a dog on heat, eh?' He laughed. 'And the Americans, always the Americans. How can he be approached? How can he speak to his old friend Josef? Is not possible.'

'So you haven't?'

Josef puffed on his cigar, an emperor on his terrace contemplating the Bay of Naples. Charles was contemplating his explanation to Hookey.

'Yet we speak. More than we speak. We meet, we drink, we embrace, we are friends, like in the camps.'

'What did you say? What did he say?'

'You have no idea what it was like, the camp.'

'How did you meet? Where?'

'Everything was different there.'

'We must leave tomorrow?' asked Yvette. She stood with a rose in one hand, a bottle in the other.

'You want to hear what he say, what I say? I tell you,' said Josef.

It took the better part of an hour. Yvette fell asleep on the floor by the window, propped up against the radiator, rose and bottle in her lap. Josef's account was punctuated by frequent visits to the toilet, after each of which he had to be led like a stubborn pony back to the point where he had left off. It turned out he had spent most of the previous day waiting in the lobby to see or – better – be seen by Federov on his way through. Sustained by alcohol, his vigil was eventually rewarded at about six in the evening when Federov hurried through on his way out, surrounded by the usual bevy of officials. Josef started up to greet him – 'I was going to shout and embrace before every-one, there was no other possibility to meet' – but was impeded by the coffee table and its cups and glasses. 'First they want to throw me out – I insist I am guest – then they clear up and put sticking plaster on my hand. But Federov is gone and I think I am never going to see him. And Yvette tells me, you are never going to meet him, it is impossible. So we eat and have more drink and I am despairing. You know this feeling, Mr Thoroughgood? Like in the camps. But then – please, please, you must drink. I am drinking. It is not polite, Mr Thoroughgood, not to drink, even for English.'

Charles poured them both more champagne and heard how, later that night, Josef and Yvette were awoken by Federov coming into their room. 'It was late, after the middle, everyone sleeps except for Federov because he has seen me in the lobby when the table hit me and he find my room number and come to me when all his people are sleeping. And we talk and we laugh and we drink until morning and Yvette is sick and we are friends again. And he will meet you.'

'You mentioned me?'

'He needs medicines, he needs treatment. His heart. He has it in Moscow, of course, special for Party members, but it is better in England. Only in England or America can he be saved, he says. But he does not know how he can be treated in London. It is expensive and he would not be permitted to come to England for that. So I tell him, I – I, Josef – can fix.' Josef grinned and struck his chest with his fist. 'I tell him my friend Mr Thoroughgood will fix. He ask if you are good doctor. I tell him you are better, you are MI6. You can command doctors.'

'He agreed to meet me?'

'In England. He is going there tomorrow. I tell him you will find him.'

'But he definitely agreed? He agreed to be in contact with MI6?'

'But he will not spy. He tell me, tell them I will not be spy. No matter, I say, they help you anyway. Is good, eh? Josef does well?'

'More than well, Josef, more than well.' Charles could imagine the reaction back in Head Office. This constituted an approach to a foreign official, which, if it went wrong, could have serious political consequences. It should have had Foreign Office clearance in advance and, as it had happened in Paris, the approval of the ambassador.

Josef struggled to his feet. 'Now we have dinner, you and me. Yvette sleeps. Somewhere where are girls, nice girls.' He grinned and his eyes disappeared in creases.

Chapter Seven

The 1980s

Hookey got up from his chair and went to the window overlooking Waterloo station. The platforms were packed with evening commuters but there were no trains. He pushed his fists into the pockets of his green cardigan, stretching it. 'So he has your real name, has been told you're MI6 and has already been introduced to you by mischance, though he wouldn't know it was that. He is expecting you to contact him here. The ambassador has expressly forbidden us to go anywhere near him and would undoubtedly be supported by the Foreign Office, which regards him as too big a fish for us to tickle. If it went wrong it could lead to public fuss, loss of any chance of aero contracts, jobs and all the rest of it. The Paris station does not know about the approach and neither does their controller, C/Europe, who will not be pleased. Meanwhile, the access agent you were supposed to have terminated has run up a breathtaking bill at the George the Fifth, which I shall have to justify. And, depending on what happens to the case – especially if nothing does – you must be considered Sovbloc Amber, which means probably blown to the Russians. More likely Sovbloc Red, certainly blown. This, of course, restricts your future postings and career. Taken together, it adds up to a bloody great cock-up.'

Hookey continued addressing the window, his tone more dispassionate than angry. 'But it's the kind of cock-up I like.' He turned back to Charles, grinning. 'Didn't Churchill say something to the effect that mistakes made facing the enemy should always be forgiven? Thing is, how to take it forward.' He began pacing the room.

'He said he won't spy,' said Charles.

'Of course he did, he has to say that. Especially in front of your agent, he'd be mad to do otherwise. But look at his background. He was condemned to hell but somehow climbed all the way back up to heaven. He can only have done that by being useful to people in power, which will have meant betraying other people in power. A dangerous game, so he's a risk-taker whose loyalty will always and only have been to the next rung he can reach. He will know that if he meets you there has to be a quid pro quo. That's how he's survived, how he's thrived, the only law he knows. He'll also know that a clandestine meeting with an officer of a hostile intelligence service would seal his fate forever, if it became known, even if it's only to discuss last year's

Dutch tulip crop. It's the agreement to meet that's the really big step, and he's taken it. Everything flows from that.' He glanced again at the window. 'Something wrong with those damn trains today.'

'It must depend a bit on whether we can get him the treatment he needs.'

'He'll assume that. People who live under totalitarian regimes in which the organs of state security are all-powerful can never believe that in democracies we keep to the law and have no executive authority. Nor would we – should we – want it. We have to find him a doctor discreetly but we'll manage that. It's what we're good at, finding and fixing things. No, it's the two river crossings we've got to manage.'

His glance betrayed some pleasure at Charles's puzzlement. 'The second is the easier, though still not easy: getting you alongside him without anyone knowing. We'll need help from SV, surveillance, which in UK ops effectively means using MI5. Which means bringing them in on it. Constitutionally, we should anyway. It's no bad thing that you're already helping them out by letting them use your flat as an LP. How's that going, by the way?'

'They're still talking about it.'

'They're good at that. See if you can blow some wind in their sails, get it moving, remind them how helpful you are.' He sat and wrote something on another solitary blank sheet of paper. 'Our first river crossing is more heavily defended. By our own side. The Foreign

Office will fight tooth and nail over this one, all the way up to the Foreign Secretary and I can't see him siding with us. Nor is it a big enough case to go to the PM, who'd probably also say no. A full-frontal assault will fail. We need a flanking movement.'

'You mean, not ask—'

'I mean MI5, again. As a joint operation with them this could be cleared through their system, which has more latitude than ours, not least because their DG is the only person with statutory authority for determining what is and is not a threat to national security. That means he can go further than we can before seeking ministerial clearance in order to establish whether or not there are grounds for acting against a threat. John Kent, their Director K Branch under whom this falls, can authorise approaches without prior clearance if he deems it necessary. D'you know him?'

'He talked to our training course. We got the impression he's rather anti-SIS.'

Hookey nodded. 'Yes, but not mortally. Just sometimes rather sceptical about us rushing into things, making exaggerated claims about the likely product, causing trouble which others have to clear up and then getting away with it scot-free. Not always entirely wrongly. I'll have a chat with him.'

'You think he'll agree?'

'We were POWs together in Italy. Camp friendships count more than most. Thought you might have learned that.' Hookey smiled briefly again. 'Now go and get on with becoming an LP. Give them reason to be grateful.'

Two hours later, Sue, the MI5 desk officer for Russian Illegals, walked from room to room, inspecting Charles's flat, sipping tea. 'Tidy and clean. For a bloke.'

'I haven't been back long. The tenant had it cleaned. It'll get worse.'

'It might have to. If you could mess it up a bit, dump some junk around the place to make it easier for Steve and the team to hide their technical clobber.'

'I could probably manage that.'

He followed her with his own mug of tea. They stood in his bedroom door, staring at the bed, mutually conscious of potential and availability. Janet had left a pair of shoes beneath one of the bedside chairs. He was to see her later.

'Is the layout of the Turnips' flat the same as this?' Sue asked. 'I'm thinking in terms of where the probes should go, where they're most likely to talk. Bedrooms aren't usually all that rewarding, despite what people think. Pillow talk doesn't often involve an exchange of nuclear secrets.' Her eyes rested for a moment on Janet's shoes. 'More the usual things.'

'My girlfriend's,' said Charles, 'not mine.'

She smiled. 'Not cheap, either.' They stood in the hall. 'There's a telephone point here but your phone has been moved into the kitchen. No idea whether theirs is the same?'

Charles shook his head. 'Why does it make a difference where the phone is if you're tapping it?'

'We're not just doing that. Steve and his merry men turn phones into microphones so they pick up everything in the room whether or not they're being used.'

'I could do a recce, knock on their door with a bottle, neighbourly greeting of new neighbours, and hope to be invited in.'

'That would be helpful, but not while I'm here. Better they didn't see me.'

She told him more about the Turnips. 'The Melburys, I should call them, otherwise you'll be calling them Turnip to their faces.' They had registered for VAT although their turnover was well below the level at which they had to and they bought very little on which they could claim it. They had made two two-night trips to Holland in the past month. 'What would be really useful is if you could discover in advance when they're next going away. Then we could do a break-in and put the probes in through your floors without risk of them hearing.'

'You have keys that would fit?'

'We make them. But we could do with a spare set of yours for when we need access to your flat. Unless they're already on loan to the lady of the shoes, of course.' She smiled.

'In the tea caddy on the kitchen shelf. Help yourself while I get changed.'

They left the flat together, she to a hen party on the South Bank, he to a curry with Janet in Kennington, around the corner from the house she shared. Sue was talking about her friend who was giving the party when, on the flight of stairs below the Turnip flat, they ran into a couple who could only be them. They were short, round and middle-aged, he wearing a blue cotton jacket and tie, she slacks and a fawn raincoat over a high-necked sweater. They were both slightly breathless. Charles introduced himself.

The man responded promptly, with a firm handshake. 'Pleased to meet you, sir. Stephen Melbury, Diane Melbury.'

Diane's handshake was also firm. It was the natural point at which to introduce Sue but Charles skipped over it. 'Are you from America?'

'Canada,' she said. 'But don't worry, we're used to people thinking we're American over here.'

'We must get together for a drink. Meanwhile, you must let me know if I make too much noise over your head.'

She laughed. 'Not a peep so far. In fact, we thought your flat was empty.'

They stood aside to let Charles and Sue pass. 'Drop in any time, Mr Thoroughgood,' said Stephen Melbury. 'Any time.'

When they were outside Sue said, 'Just what I didn't want. Means I can't join in on any surveillance of them, which is usually the fun bit. Hope they didn't think it odd, your not introducing me.'

'I assumed you wouldn't want it. I'll give them the impression you're one of many.'

'That'll go down well with your smart-shoe lady.'

Chapter Eight

The Present

Age and child-bearing had caused Sue to put on weight over the years but she was big-boned and carried it well. She sat back and again surveyed the surroundings. It was early evening and diners were fortifying themselves with drinks before dinner. 'God, Thoroughgood, how did you worm your way into a club like this? Or does it come with the job?'

'Sadly not. Nothing does except arguments about money and a car and driver strictly for official duties only. I joined years ago. Needed somewhere to keep me off the streets.'

'Like hell you did. That lovely flat in the Boltons. What happened to it?'

'Sold on marriage.'

'Married too, of course. I heard all about that. And Chief of MI6. Not sure which looked least likely when I knew you. Jammy sod.' She smiled with the licence of former intimacy.

'It was Jam I wanted to talk to you about.'

She frowned as the waiter handed her a second glass of club dry white. 'You've got me there, I'm afraid.'

They had not seen each other for twenty or so years. Charles had to remind her of the Turnips, the case that had begun their acquaintanceship. The friendship formed then petered out when she remarried and left MI5 to have children, rejoining later when the children were older. But by then she and Charles were in different spheres and had not come across each other until he rang her that morning.

'Of course, yes,' she interrupted as he explained. 'The far-left brother of your girlfriend. Don't think I ever met him, did I? But you did, I remember your write-up. Janet, wasn't it, your girlfriend? Good taste in shoes. Did your relationship recover or was it a permanent casualty of the Turnip operation?'

'Pretty permanent. We lost touch. She married a banker.'

'Better off than with you, then. The Turnips did her a favour. So, why does the mighty C want to know about her brother?'

Charles told her of Michael Dunton's question about Deep Blue. 'I am right in thinking that's what it was, aren't I?'

'I think you are, but I don't think we ever worked out what they planned to do with it, did we? It didn't seem to fit with anything else they aspired to, like

76

bringing down the capitalist system. Unless they just wanted to cause mayhem.'

'If Michael were here I could simply ask him to get someone to check that volume of the file, the one we don't have, and then hand the case over to him. But I'm reluctant to brief Simon Mall on it because—'

'Nothing will happen.'

'Precisely. Jam and that whole episode is missing from our files because by the time he got involved it had become a joint case under Director K and all the paperwork was on your MI5 file, supposedly copied to us but that didn't always happen. I think there was a fair bit on Jam's activities at the time which may be relevant again now that he seems to be involved with Triple A. And of course a complicating factor where Simon Mall is concerned is that Melanie Stokes – now of your parish – is shacked up with Jam. Simon would be too frightened of his own shadow to go anywhere near either of them.'

Sue's eyes widened. 'But she must be twenty years younger than Jam, at least. He's an old man, isn't he? About your age.'

'Thanks. And, quite apart from Simon's legendary caution, if I approach your service officially about him it could get back to her.'

'So you want me to smuggle papers out?'

'No. It's got to be done officially, in a way that's accountable if it comes out.'

'Trouble is, the old K Branch doesn't exist any more

and all that Cold War stuff is archived. I'd have to have a reason for asking for it.'

'How about a vetting query from our vetting section? We feel we should brief Melanie Stokes now that she's doing whatever she's doing with you and wanted to check her clearances, in the course of which we've come across references to file traces on Jam, held by you. So we've asked you what they are and you've kindly dug them out and copied them to us.'

Sue's eyes widened again. 'Not bad. You might have made a half-decent MI5 officer if you'd transferred to us. Which would have spared you getting locked up by your predecessor. Tell me about that. Is it true that she ... your wife ...'

'Sarah.'

'... used to be his wife?'

Once again, Charles produced an edited version of the events that had brought him and Sarah together, though for Sue he provided more detail than usual. They reminisced until their glasses were empty again. She refused another because she had to get back to her family. 'Won't Sarah want to know where you are?'

'She works longer hours than I do.'

On the way out she paused at the top of the steps overlooking Pall Mall. 'I always felt bad about Janet. I mean, I know you and I weren't ... at that point, anyway – but because of the fact that I'd been in your flat that day and she couldn't believe there was nothing going on between us. She must have been very upset.'

'It didn't make for a good night.'

'And then we made you get back in touch with her about her brother.'

'It would have ended anyway.'

She kissed him on the cheek. 'She doesn't know how lucky she was.'

Sarah was still at work when he returned to their house in the quiet street behind Westminster Abbey. Not trusting him to choose dinner, she had left written instructions about lasagne and the microwave, with vegetables only left to his initiative. He poured more wine and began laying the table, recalling the night Sue had mentioned, the night following her visit to his flat and their meeting the Melburys on the stairs.

The 1980s

The curry in Kennington had been fine, with Janet chatting about her week and some gossip about mutual friends from Oxford. When they went to bed in his flat, however, she refused his attention, turning on her side and pulling the bedclothes almost over her head.

'I just don't want to,' she said in a small voice, resentful and stubborn.

'OK. Any reason in particular?' He propped himself up on his elbow and put his hand on her shoulder. 'Look, if there's something wrong you may as well say so. I can't do anything about it unless I know what it is.'

Her silence was heavy with the implication that he

ought not to need telling. 'You've had another woman here.'

Because he hadn't, in the sense she meant, and because he had been conscious of the possibility with Sue, his denial was too prompt and unequivocal.

'I could smell her scent when I came in. She's been in this room.'

He had an instant to decide whether to maintain his denial or whether to retract and explain – that a woman had been in the room but not in his bed, that it was a professional visit by an MI5 officer in connection with an operation he was helping with, that he wasn't in the Foreign Office at all and that he had misled her all along as to the real nature of his career.

'I haven't had any other woman here. I've not been unfaithful.'

'I don't believe you.'

It wasn't until just before dawn that they slipped into deep and independent slumbers. As it was Saturday there was no hurry to get up. Charles was awoken by knocking. He wrapped a towel around his waist and opened the door to Stephen Melbury, this time wearing checked trousers and a blazer and tie. His smile showed a mouthful of unnaturally white and even teeth. 'My apologies for disturbing you, Charles. I may call you Charles? Thank you. We're off to Kew for the day, Diane being something of a botanist, but we'd be very pleased if you could join us for a drink this evening. Along with your young lady, of course, whose name I didn't catch when we met yesterday.'

'That's very kind, Stephen, I'd love to. It'll be just me, I'm afraid.'

'Great. About seven.'

Janet was in the bathroom when he returned. He put on the kettle, loaded the toaster, laid out the cereals. She came into the kitchen fully dressed, her bag packed, her short dark hair precisely brushed, her expression determinedly neutral. 'Goodbye, Charles.'

He looked at her.

'I heard every word that man said. You've clearly had someone here. You lied to me. You've been lying all along for all I know.'

Her small regular features seemed prettier than ever now, as if clarified by determination. He went to her. 'Don't touch me,' she said.

'Look, yes, there was someone here but it's not what you think.'

'So you did lie? And now you're lying again, I'm sure.'

'Sit down. Let me explain.'

'I don't want to hear. I told you, I'm going.'

'I lied because I had to.' He told her he wasn't in the Foreign Office, that he was in MI6 and helping with an operation, that the female visitor was a work colleague assessing his flat for possible use, that it was nothing personal.

She was unmoved. 'How very convenient. But since

you've lied to me about everything else all along, I suppose it makes no difference if you lie about this too. There's no point, Charles. We – it wasn't going anywhere, anyway. There's no point. There never was. Goodbye.'

She walked out, her voice and self-control intact. He followed her to the door and called out as she descended the stone stairs but she neither paused nor answered. He respected her for that, and stood waiting to hear the front door close. Not for the first time, he was struck by how a relationship which had not felt like a burden swiftly became one in retrospect, as if it always had been. He suspected that that suggested something not very pleasant about himself, but was spared further introspection by the phone.

Hookey never bothered with preliminaries. 'Your friend is in town and I have his programme. All meetings and whatever except for this afternoon when he's going to a football match, Arsenal versus Manchester United. Keen on football, apparently, and the Foreign Office had to bust their guts to get tickets at nil notice. They've got three in the VIP box, one of which will be taken by their escorting desk officer. No idea who'll have the other but you must get there and make contact. Up to you how you do that. Five have agreed to provide a small SV team to follow him from the hotel to the ground so they can put you alongside him if there's a chance. Don't forget your shorts and dubbin for your boots. If anyone does that now.' He chuckled.

'Couldn't I just ring him at his hotel?'

'You won't know who's with him when he picks up the phone. He's got to see and recognise you and you've got to leave him with a way of contacting you. I've got you a dedicated operational number to give him which will come straight through to the switchboard here who'll put it through to you wherever you are. Ring me back when we've finished speaking and I'll give it to you in a separate call, along with another number which is a Five number for you to RV with SV. OK?'

'Does the Foreign Office—'

'Not yet but they will. Won't be best pleased, of course. Don't suppose you know anyone with any VIP box tickets you could scrounge?'

'No, I—'

'Well, good luck, old son. I shall be sailing in Suffolk this afternoon, contactable this evening. Ring as soon as you've got news.'

Charles shaved and showered, breakfasting at the table he had laid for two. He was tempted to ring Janet and say sorry. Sorry for what, she might ask? Being what he was, principally, and since he wasn't going to do anything about that, there wasn't much point in apologising. He still wanted her to know that he hadn't been lying. Yet, essentially, he had. The lie was in allowing her to think he might want her more than he did, and in taking advantage of that. Spying, which people associated with lying, was relatively

ALAN JUDD

straightforward and clear: you lied for truth, you deceived in order to discover hidden truth. It was in his personal life that the distinction became blurred, too deeply embedded to disentangle. He would have to report to the Office that he'd made her conscious to himself as SIS, and why. It would go on his security file.

'Farther to your left, next entrance but one. VIP entrance. They're heading for it now.'

Brian cocked his head to listen before murmuring into the lapel of his donkey jacket. 'We've just come from there. Must've passed them. Sure it's them?'

'Walking three abreast. Target in the middle. Just passed the hot dogs.'

'On our way.'

Brian nodded to Charles and they turned about. It was not easy to cut across the crowd streaming into the stadium. They had followed Federov and his party in cars from their hotel, a straightforward job until the Russians left the Foreign Office car and driver some streets away and joined the crowds on foot. The fast-moving crush made it difficult to keep them in sight without getting too close. The aim was to position Charles close enough to speak to Federov if he became separated, however briefly, without being noticed by the two others.

They found the trio as they joined the short queue for the VIP entrance. Federov wore a smart camel coat and a black fur hat. His embassy colleague, a balding, sad-looking man, wore a grey raincoat. Their Foreign Office liaison, wearing jacket and jumper with no tie, was looking uneasily about him as if unsure they were in the right queue.

'Want to be in the queue behind them?' asked Brian.

Charles nodded. 'Not too close.' He had no idea what he would do, just that he had to be close enough to take advantage of any opportunity that offered. That happened unexpectedly quickly. The liaison desk officer, looking increasingly anxious, rifled through his jacket pockets. He stopped moving with the rest of the queue, the others stopped with him, and the people behind moved round them. Charles and Brian had to do the same and found themselves approaching the barrier sooner than Charles wanted. There were only four or five people ahead when the Foreign Office man found the tickets and his party rejoined the queue behind. As he approached the barrier Charles slowed and looked obviously about him. 'Still no sign of Pete,' he said, loudly enough to be heard. 'We'll have to step aside if he doesn't come. Won't get in without his ticket.'

Brian caught on. 'Can't you leave it with the blokes at the turnstile?'

'Doubt it.' Charles made sure his gaze traversed those behind him. The Foreign Office man was passing a ticket to Federov's colleague. Both had their eyes down. Charles caught Federov's eye. It was only a moment but there was recognition, and uncertainty. Charles looked away as the queue moved forward. They were next but two now. He felt in his jacket pocket for the slip of paper with the operational number, then turned back again and, addressing Brian, pointed across and behind them. 'Isn't that him over there? Bloody idiot, what's he doing? Look at him.'

His straightened arm was an inch or two from the Foreign Office man's nose. For a couple of seconds all those behind looked where Charles was pointing. He stepped backwards out of the queue and slipped the paper into Federov's coat pocket. 'He's going the other way, the bloody fool. Better get after him.' He and Brian hurried away.

'Hope he knows you've stuck it on him,' said Brian.

'I gave a tug at his pocket. I was worried someone might think I was picking it.'

'I was going to offer to feign a heart attack at the turnstile. Had to do that once in Leicester Square. Worked a treat except that I had to spend half the night in A and E.'

They headed for the team's cars, parked some streets away, making slow progress against the tide. Charles thought they must be the only ones heading away from the ground until his eye was caught by another couple on the other side of the road, moving slowly against the high stadium wall, in parallel and slightly ahead. It was difficult to see them clearly because of the teeming people between and because they were both short.

'Slow down,' he said to Brian. 'Couple ahead on the other side of the road, against the wall, going our way.'

'Clocked them. The bloody Turnips. We was on them two days ago. Lot of hanging around for nothing. They haven't come for the football, no more than we have. Know them, do you?'

'My neighbours. I'm helping with the operation.'

'Stop here and turn round, so your back's to them.' They stood by someone's rickety garden gate. Brian took out his wallet. 'You're a tout and I'm buying a ticket. We'll keep talking all the time I've got them in view. They're up to something. Not looking across. It's the wall they're interested in.' He spoke into his lapel, guiding the foot team that had put them on to Federov to move in ahead of the Turnips. 'We'll keep them in view till the others are on to them,' he said. 'Then we'll drop out, since they know you.'

Charles, keeping his back to them, took out his own wallet and pretended to search through it.

'Iron stanchion up against the wall,' said Brian. 'They've stopped by it. She's looking in her handbag. Bugger, people in the way. We'll have to—' He broke off, tilting his head again. 'OK, the others have clocked them now. They've moving off, same direction but faster. They've done something, done a drop, I bet. Or cleared one. Hang on till they're out of sight, then we'll have a butcher's.'

The crowd was thinning, with latecomers walking more rapidly. The other team reported that the Turnips were heading purposefully towards the underground station. They went over to the great metal stanchion, which was almost as high as the stadium wall and bolted flat against it. The stragglers hurried past unnoticing as Brian inspected it closely.

'Gap about shoulder height, see? Just enough for an envelope but it wouldn't slip down because of the bolts beneath. Can't see it unless you're right up against the wall as I am, and she was. DLB, bet my bottom dollar.'

Charles had never seen a dead letter box used in anger, only on exercises. 'Won't they have left a signal to show they've emptied it?'

'Probably but maybe not here. Safer to leave it somewhere else.'

'There's a chalk mark on the wall, look, about ten yards away.' There was a single vertical line about six inches long.

'That's just where she was standing when he put his hand on her shoulder after they'd moved away. Too close, really, that mark. Not good tradecraft. Pity they've emptied it rather than filled it. The other way round we'd have had whoever it's for.'

'Better move, hadn't we? In case whoever it's for comes back to check.'

'Guess so, though it could be days before he does. Wouldn't have to come right here, he could see it from a car driving past.'

They headed back towards their own car. Brian's

lapel reported that the Turnips were on the tube, surveillance still with them. There was a roar from the
stadium. 'Arsenal one down already, I bet,' he said.

'You'll report to Sue, the desk officer?'

'First thing Monday. No point calling her out now,
the action's happened. Anyway, they don't like weekend work, desk officers. Not like us lucky sods.'

Charles refused the offer of a lift back to his flat in
case the Turnips saw him being dropped off. Instead,
they dropped him near Piccadilly Circus to pick up
a tube to South Kensington. The station was closed
because of an IRA bomb scare so he walked back,
musing on whether he should send flowers to Janet.
Or take them. But, unable to explain to himself precisely why he would be doing it, and feeling it would
compound his essential dishonesty, he did neither. He
thought of ringing her when he got back to the flat but
changed his mind and rang the Office switchboard.
They put him through to the MI5 switchboard and he
left a message for Sue to ring him in not less than an
hour. He used that time to go for a run over the King's
Road and down to the river.

She rang as he got in the door, panting. 'No good
ringing me about heart attacks, if that's what you're
having,' she said. He described what had happened.
'Did you get any photos?'

'Not of the DLB episode. The other team may have
taken some, later.'

'Pity, they're useful evidence. But what good news,

well spotted. Interesting to hear what they have to say about their afternoon in Kew.'

He went down to their flat that evening with a welcoming bottle of champagne, unsure whether that was too obviously overdoing it or whether it was claimable as an operational expense. He compromised by taking as cheap a bottle as he could find, then felt uneasy about that.

Stephen Melbury opened the door wide, with a smile to match. 'I like a man who's punctual, Charlie.' He held on to Charles's hand. 'Forgive me, I should sort this out now. Are you Charles or Charlie?'

Charles hated Charlie. 'Usually, Charles but I answer to either.'

'That's fine. It's like my name, Stephen or Steve. Mostly, I'm Steve, but no big issue.' He took the proffered champagne. 'Hey, you didn't need to do this. Hey, sweetie, look what Charlie's brought us. Puts us to shame.'

Diane emerged from the kitchen with bowls of crisps and peanuts. She was wearing glasses this time. 'Oh my, what a treat. We should open it right now. It's better than the wine we've got.'

'I'll do it. You take him through, sweetie, keep him going on nuts and crisps till I come with the bubbles.'

Their flat was larger than his, with two bedrooms, and differently configured. All rooms opened off a long hall with fitted bookshelves. The kitchen, at the far end, was more or less under his but bigger. The sitting room was on the left, facing the road and furnished with two armchairs, a sofa, a folding table and television. Along the near wall packing cases were stacked shoulder-height.

'Sorry about the mess,' said Diane. 'It's books, books, books with us. The spare bedroom is full of them and until we get more shelves up the overflow is in here.'

Steve appeared with the champagne and glasses on a tray. 'How long have you lived here, Charlie?' He laughed. 'Sorry, Charles.'

Conversation flowed predictably, with polite questions about Charles's background and life and no sign of undue interest when he trotted out his usual Foreign Office cover as a desk officer in the Southern Africa Department. He in turn asked polite questions about the book business and why they had left Canada: 'We figured London's a bigger market and once you get known here you get to hear of things before they come on to the market.' Their cover was as uncontentious and well-rehearsed as his own, he reflected, confident that if he asked they would doubtless talk convincingly about sales and purchases just as he could say which room he notionally worked in, name his colleagues and talk with seeming authority about African affairs.

'How was Kew?' he asked, holding out his glass for a refill.

'Wonderful, just wonderful,' Diane said promptly.

'I've not seen anything like it in the whole of Canada. In fact, I'm not sure there is anything like Kew anywhere.'

'Diane is into plants,' said Steve. 'Big time.'

'But not you?'

'Me? Sure, I like them, like looking at them. But I don't know what I'm looking at and she tells me and I forget. Goes right out of my head. I got no head for plants. And you?'

'In your camp, I'm afraid.'

'Wonderful, those glasshouses they got there, just wonderful.'

'Easy journey, too.'

'Fine, fine, no problem on those trains. Diane specialises in rare books and plants. That's her speciality.'

'Since I was eight,' she said. 'That's when I got interested.'

It would have been easy to say they'd changed their minds about Kew, had tried to go to a football match instead but couldn't get in. Anything clandestine was always best interleaved with truth in case chance or a watchful security service caught you out, as now.. Eventually, after more talk about London and its transport problems, he said he'd better go.

'Off out tonight, Charlie? Saturday night with a great city like London at your feet?'

'Doing something with your girlfriend?' asked Diane.

'Not tonight, I'm afraid. Early night for once.'

'She's some girl. I wouldn't let her out of my sight if I were you.'

He took his time leaving, trying to note the placing of furniture and concluding that the phone must be in the kitchen. As soon as he was back in his flat he sketched everything he remembered and reconciled himself to the early night he had predicted. That at least was true.

Chapter Nine

The Present

When the house phone rang in Cowley Street that night Charles had to search for it, so rarely was it used. He answered without checking the number, assuming it was Sarah, working even later than usual. But it was Melanie Stokes.

'Charles, hi. So glad I caught you. Something else I meant to say but it clean went out of my head when we met at the NSC the other day. We were being so serious and work-orientated.' She laughed. 'Are you and your wife – Sarah, isn't it? – free to come to dinner on Friday?' She left him no time to reply. 'I do hope so because James, my partner, is an old friend of yours and he's dying to meet up again.'

That was hard to believe but Charles pretended not to know who James was, simulated pleasure when she told him and said he would need to check with Sarah. Marriage had its uses. Although, the more he thought about it, the more he was inclined to accept.

'Do hope you can, it would be so lovely to meet Sarah. Nothing formal, just a kitchen table supper. We're not a million miles from you. Notting Hill.'

She had got his number from MI5, she told him. 'You must give me your mobile. They didn't have that.' Sarah's name she could have got by googling him.

When Sarah got home she pulled a face at the news. 'I was going to suggest we go down to Swinbrook on Friday night. The house really needs using, at least heating up a bit. I suppose we could go straight on afterwards, if it's not too late? I'm surprised you want to see them, given what you've said about the Wicked Witch.'

'I don't, but there'll be a reason she's doing it and I'd like to know what it is. It won't be purely social.'

'Were you friends with her partner?'

'Hardly, but we knew each other. He used to think I was a stuck-up fascist pig. I went out with his sister.'

'Another one I haven't heard about?'

'On the rebound from you, as it happens. He's called James Micklethwaite and he used to be deep into the Campaign for Nuclear Disarmament as well as some other anarchist outfit. Now he's mixed up with Triple A.'

She looked up from the pile of circulars and special offers on the kitchen table. 'James Micklethwaite. That's the man who was emailing me before I offloaded the Triple A case. Kept saying how much they were looking forward to working with me. He writes literate emails, better than most of my clients. Is it wise, mixing with people like him, in your position?'

'Probably not, but there's something I want to find out.'

'I don't think you should go. We can get out of it. Just say we're going to Swinbrook.'

'It's to do with an old case and something called Deep Blue. Somehow. Except that I'm not sure how it all fits. That's what I want to find out.'

'Your passion for the past will be the undoing of you, Charles Thoroughgood.'

'It got me married to you.'

Smiling, she swept the circulars into the bin. 'Maybe that's what I mean.'

Lying awake again that night, waiting for Big Ben to strike, he tried to recall every detail of that other night many years ago, the one following the brush contact outside Arsenal's old stadium and his drink with the Melburys.

The 1980s

He had been in a deep sleep – he slept better in those days – when roused by his phone at 1.10 a.m. It was in the kitchen and he got up without switching on the light, blundering into the doorpost in the dark. At first, no one spoke, then a voice, quiet and accented, said, 'This is Igor. I am in room four-six-seven. We can meet now. Do not ask at reception. You know hotel?'

'I'll be there in thirty minutes.'

There was no point in rousing Hookey, assuming he ever went to bed. He could only say, hear what he has to say, make no commitments and report back. Charles took pen and notepaper and cash for a taxi. It might have been quicker to drive but parking in Kensington was difficult. Anyway, he might have to drink a lot.

Kensington in the early hours seemed no less busy than at any other time. The hotel was one often used by the Russian Embassy for visitors. There was no trouble with reception because it was thronged with drunken Welshmen singing 'Guide Me, O Thou Great Redeemer'. Their rugby team had triumphed at Twickenham that day, a game Charles would normally have watched. He slipped through unnoticed, took a lift to the ninth floor and walked down the fire escape to the fourth. The corridor was carpeted and silent. Federov's colleagues would be in rooms nearby so he would have to knock softly, but there was no need. The door to room 467 was slightly ajar. He paused, listening for voices, then stepped in.

Federov was sitting at the desk, writing. He wore a light-grey suit and did not look up until Charles had closed and locked the door. Then he stood and walked over, unsmiling, with outstretched hand. They shook and he gestured Charles to the nearer armchair. He took the other. Neither had spoken.

'How can we help you?' asked Charles.

Federov's moist dark eyes rested on Charles. Everything in the room was neat, ordered, contained, pyjamas folded, closed suitcase on the luggage stand, closed briefcase by the desk, papers neatly arranged. Uniquely, in Charles's experience of Russian officials, there was no sign of a drink apart from a glass of water on the desk. The corner tray of cups and kettle was untouched.

'Probably you cannot.' Federov paused. 'My heart is failing. Drugs can help but the doctors say I need a new heart. They could give me one in Moscow but really they have little success with such operations. They say the best doctors for this are here in London but it is very expensive. Also, it is difficult for Soviet officials to come here for medical treatment.'

'Your government would not permit it?'

Federov raised one hand from the arm of his chair and shook his head. 'Sometimes it is possible to arrange things.'

Although the gesture was economical and contained, like everything else about Federov, it reminded Charles of Josef's extravagant protestations that everything and everyone in the Soviet Union was for sale.

'But your security people—'

'The problems are here, with you, with your Foreign Office. They would not give me visa. Just as we would not give them visa for such a thing.'

'Have you tried?'

'I do not want to risk refusal.'

'You would like MI6 to try to arrange it? To use our influence?' Charles's choice of words was deliberate. Federov was unlikely to harbour any illusions but it was important to make clear that he was dealing with an intelligence service, not an individual or a public department of state.

He nodded, once.

'I can find out. If we were able to help, how would you explain it to your people?'

'You must please understand, Mr Thoroughgood, that in Russia we live two lives, parallel lives. One life is our official life in which we speak and act correctly as good communists. Our other life is the life of how things work. I have done many important people many good favours, helpful things. If I ask a favour, it is usually granted.'

It felt like dealing with another intelligence officer. Federov was not one but as a Party apparatchik and Central Committee member he knew how to work a system, how to trade. He would expect to pay a price. If this was to be considered a recruitment, it was the most relaxing one Charles had achieved so far, with no need to court or cultivate, to flatter, to cajole, to be circumspect. It was refreshingly honest. 'You understand that we would expect something in return,' he said.

'State secrets. You want state secrets.'

'And a regular professional relationship, meeting you whenever possible.'

'Not in Moscow.'

'When you come out, when you travel.'

'What kind of secrets? Political secrets? Military secrets? Intelligence secrets? I am not member of special services.'

'You know people who are, people who talk to you. You are on the Central Committee, you know people in the Politburo, you hear about policies—'

'Josef has told you this?' Federov smiled for the first time, shaking his head. 'He exaggerates.'

'We would want to know everything you know.'

'And you would want me to tell you secrets first, before I have new heart. Because if I am better you might never see me again. But if I have told you something, you have hold on me. Yes?'

'We want you to speak to us willingly and honestly.'

'An honest spy?'

'Yes.' This time they both smiled.

'And if I say no you will chase after me with your questions, try to blackmail me?'

'No. But you have my number in case you change your mind.'

'Josef would know. And his wife.'

'They don't know we're meeting. We could tell them we couldn't get near you, or that we did but you refused. On the other hand, they could be very useful if they knew because we could make contact arrangements through them.'

'Who else would know?'

'My boss. And C, the Chief of MI6.'

'And your boss's secretary and your Chief's secretary and the filing clerks who keep my file. And other people.'

It was true. Even the most restricted cases were always known to at least a handful of people. If not always the agent's name, enough for an effective counter-intelligence service to work it out. 'They would know about your case but not necessarily your identity. You would be referred to only by a code-name or number. Even in Head Office here in London no one would say your name aloud.'

There was a pause. 'You do not ask why I am doing this.'

'Your heart.'

'That is part, yes. But nothing else, do you believe?'

Looking at the impassive features and dark, steady gaze, Charles realised that they perhaps concealed more than they revealed. 'You want me to guess your motives?'

'That is part of your job, is it not? Always to assess, to decide whether I am true and not a double agent, I think you call it?' He smiled, very slightly. 'I wish to know what you think of me.'

Charles hesitated. Agent motivation usually involved a plurality of motives, variable over time and context. Federov was an intelligent man who would be insulted by something glib from the training manual, or perhaps put off by too penetrating an analysis, supposing Charles were capable of it. 'I once read of a fourteenth-century English judge who, asked to decide whether someone had really intended to commit a crime, declared, "The devil alone knoweth the heart of man." You are asking me to read what is in your heart.'

'I ask your opinion, that is all.'

Charles hesitated again. If he got it badly wrong the case would be stillborn. He remembered what Josef had said about people released from the camps. 'I think you've had enough and want to get your own back.'

'Get my own back? Explain, please.'

'To get revenge for what happened when you were young. Sent to prison for no good reason.'

Federov nodded slowly. 'Ten years, yes, the penalty for doing nothing. More if you had done something. That is partly true. What else, do you think?'

Charles smiled. 'I'm not a psychoanalyst. You tell me.'

'If I spy for you and I am in danger of being discovered or if I have nothing more to spy on, I should wish to retire here in England with my family. To defect, I think you call it.'

This was a decision for the Home Office and Foreign Office on recommendation from the defectors subcommittee. An open-ended commitment such as Federov wanted was most unusual and should in no circumstances be given without clearance. Charles struggled to remain a good bureaucrat. 'If you work for us honestly and successfully, we can recommend it. Our recommendation will be taken seriously but I can't promise an answer in advance.'

'Of course you can make no commitment. I understand that.' His face darkened. 'But your organisation must also understand something. You are asking me to risk my life and the liberty and future of my family for a maybe, a perhaps, a possible. That is not enough. Do you understand that?'

Clearly, this was make or break. 'I do understand. I agree. I promise.'

'You promise. What? To make a recommendation?'

'I promise that provided you work for us and give good information you will be able to defect with your family.' He would consider later how to present this in Head Office.

Federov stared for a long moment, then stood and held out his hand. 'I will take your word as a gentleman, Mr Thoroughgood. The word of MI6.'

It was important not to show embarrassment at this unwonted formality. Charles stood and solemnly shook hands. 'But I must take back some indication of what you can do for us,' he said as they sat.

'Of course. Is it sufficient if I tell you that your government's attempts to sell Rolls-Royce engines for our civil aircraft cannot work? It is decided already that we will buy the French and my delegation is here only to show politeness and so that we can see London. The reason is not that the French engines are better but that we have a special relationship with the French minister of aviation, who will benefit privately. Your government may not like this but they will be interested, I think.'

'Thank you, Igor, they will. One question: do you know of any penetration of any part of the British government or other NATO countries by Russian special services?' It was always the first question, the one that had to be asked.

'You mean, do I know anyone here who spy for KGB?' He smiled and shook his head. 'I told you, I am not familiar with their secrets. I know people in the organs of state security, I can tell you about them, but they do not tell me their secrets.'

'But you'll tell me if they do?'

He stood and came over to Charles, patting his shoulder paternally. 'Do not worry, Mr Thoroughgood. If you give me new heart, I give you all I can.'

They agreed future contact arrangements. Charles was to get details of a heart consultant whom MI6 trusted, Federov was to ring the operational number for the details, then contact the consultant himself and arrange to come out again.

As he walked back along the silent corridor, Charles was still unsure. Security Branch would say it was all too easy, too pat; everything known about Federov suggested a man prepared to betray anyone and everyone, he would have no compunction about leading on MI6 to get what he wanted while simultaneously reinsuring himself with the KGB. They in turn would probably be happy to play him back, using him to find out what we wanted to know, where our gaps were. They had a rich history of double-agent operations dating from Lenin's time and, unlike Western services, were prepared to play them long. They would give their DAs real intelligence rather than the obvious chickenfeed which Western agencies gave to theirs. This was, after all, a culture that had sacrificed tens of thousands of soldiers during the Second World War in order to persuade the Germans that their star agent was loyal, rather than the KGB double agent he really was. Federov might get a new heart, Security would say, but his head would stay the same and he would have to deliver very significantly to persuade Security Branch that that had changed. They would not yet consider him an agent.

Chapter Ten

The Present

Dinner with Melanie was not at her flat but in a crowded Italian restaurant near Notting Hill underground, where the staff knew her. She and James were there already.

'I just couldn't get away in time to do anything, so hope you don't mind it's not *chez nous*,' she said, presenting her cheek for Charles as if they were old friends. Her perfume was strong and her hair smelled as if it needed washing. She shook hands with Sarah. 'I've been longing to meet you, having read so much about you. You're easily the most talked-about couple in the intelligence community.'

They shook hands with James, who did not stand. His handshake was warm and limp. Charles could have passed him on the street without knowing him. He had lost most of his hair and put on considerable weight. His features – the snub nose, the delicate eyebrows, something about the mouth – were recognisable, reminiscent of his sister's, but his face had widened and his skin coarsened. He was fashionably unshaved. His manner with them both was at first almost diffident, lacking the vociferous angry sarcasm of the youthful Jam, but as the meal went on diffidence came to seem more the contemptuous reserve of one who feels that contributing is beneath him.

'Long time since we last did this,' said Charles.

'Not sure we ever did, did we?'

For most of the first course Melanie interrogated Sarah about her job, showing some insight and affecting great interest in the foibles of private client work. James answered Charles's questions about his sister without resistance or enthusiasm. They didn't see much of each other, she'd married her American banker in London, had given up her job to return with him to New York, had two children, came over now and again to see their widowed mother, seemed OK. 'Got the kind of life she wants.'

'And what have you done since those days?'

James shrugged as if the question were beneath him. 'This and that. Crusading for a fairer and more equal world. Not the sort of thing that would interest you.' He half smiled. 'But you probably know all about what I've been doing, being where you are now.'

'Not my business. Nor anyone else's in my world. We don't do British politics.'

'Not even the SNP? Breaking up the United

Kingdom and all that? That's a threat to national security, surely?'

'Not even the SNP. Anyone who submits themselves to the ballot box, unless they're doing something illegal, is off our radar. But you're not SNP, are you? They're not radical enough for you, are they?'

'Hypothetical example. Not a drop of Scottish blood in the Micklethwaites.' His tone became more aggressive. 'Must be interesting, the stuff you see, hard to resist, trawling through everyone's texts and emails, listening to their calls. Listen to mine, do you?'

This was wearily familiar territory. 'No, Jam, I don't. I'm sorry to say, you're of no intelligence interest, like ninety-nine-point-nine-nine-nine per cent of mankind. In fact, I don't listen to anyone's calls or read anyone's emails. And even if we were interested and legally per-mitted and had several hundred thousand staff to read and listen to them all, we'd be driven mad with boredom.'

'But you still have the power to listen to those you want to listen to.'

'Not without legitimate reason.'

'And who says it's legitimate?'

'The independent overseers, judges.'

'But how do we know you're not fooling them, making it up?'

Charles shrugged. The impossibility of proving negatives was something that came with the job. 'Too many people would know. It would be bound to come to light and someone would blow the whistle.'

'You could have them killed, stuffed in a sports bag in Pimlico to make it look like some kinky accident.'

He knew James to be an intelligent man who in any other area of life would be sceptical to the point of cynicism, but he was one of those for whom the supposed activities of British intelligence agencies prompted an immediate suspension of disbelief, a naïve credulity that countenanced anything discreditable while denying anything good. What concerned Charles was whether this assumption of ill-will in others would justify, for James, acts as crass as those he imputed to the forces of evil.

He smiled and shook his head. 'That's like me assuming you're tunnelling under Downing Street to blow up the cabinet because you can't prove you're not.'

James smiled in return. 'That might be more justifiable.'

They were interrupted by the arrival of the main course. Melanie turned her attention to Charles. 'Any further news of office moves? We've heard nothing. Peter – Home Sec Peter – thinks the Treasury may be trying to put the kybosh on office moves unless they can be shown to save money.'

She focused on any man she spoke to as if there were no one else in the room, especially women. Her attention concentrated like a searchlight, leaving Sarah in darkness. James also ignored Sarah, absorbed in his lasagne; Charles remembered now that he never had been one for speaking while eating, stopping mid-sentence when food was placed before him and resuming only when his plate was clean. His own efforts to address both women did nothing to diffuse Melanie's concentrated beam. She finished every question or remark with a smile, regardless of subject. After ten minutes of probing his opinions of Whitehall personalities, by which time Sarah had finished her Caesar salad and James had emptied the last of the wine into his own glass, Charles felt fed up and reckless enough to fire off a flare to see if anything moved.

'How about MI5's investigations into Triple A? Any serious subversion or just the usual political stuff, tax-and-spend-our-way-to-paradise?'

'They don't do subversion. It says so on the website. Subversion's Cold War old hat.' This time there was no smile.

'Except for those still fighting it,' said James.

'I got the impression from Michael Dunton that he was worried about the outer fringes of Triple A, people plotting direct action, that kind of thing.'

'What do you mean by direct action?' asked James. 'What kind of thing?'

Charles saw Melanie glance warily, almost anxiously, at him. 'I don't know. Anything from occupations and riots, the usual thing, to acts of sabotage, maybe, or kidnappings.'

'Public-order stuff, police stuff, nothing to do with us,' said Melanie. She held up her hand for more wine.

'Now tell me how you two got together. Is everything I've read about it true?' The smile returned.

Over coffee and more wine they rehearsed the expurgated-for-public-consumption version of their story: of their early relationship as students, Sarah's marriage to their mutual friend who became Chief of the short-lived Intelligence Services Agency, his disgrace and death, their subsequent marriage and Charles's surprise appointment as Chief of the reinstated MI6. Neither liked having to do it but both accepted it as an inevitable consequence of remaining in the Whitehall world.

'All worked out pretty well for you both, then?' said James. 'Convenient, too, having a lawyer in the family, given Charles's job.'

'Sorting out the wills and estates of the rich is not much use to Charles, I'm afraid,' said Sarah.

'How are you finding the world of counter-terrorism?' Charles asked Melanie. 'Plenty of work about?'

'I think they – we – seem to have things pretty much under control at present. It was a surprise to me how much goes on. But anything can happen, of course.'

'And one day it will.'

'What makes you say that?' asked James.

'Because things do, that's all. Not always what we think or in the way we think.'

James stared for a few seconds, then folded his arms, sat back and gazed around the room with apparent indifference. They discussed trends in terrorism until the bill came. The hubbub in the restaurant rendered lowered voices unnecessary and impractical, but even so Melanie's clear and energetic high-pitch carried. She thought the main threat was no longer home-grown but would come from what she called transcontinental incomers. 'We're too hung up on spying on our own people. We must steer clear from legitimate protest and place our shields according to where the arrows come from.' She insisted on paying.

They lingered on the pavement outside. Charles and Sarah had to explain that they had come by car because they were heading off to Sarah's Cotswold house.

'Very nice,' said James. He pointed to a blue Bentley parked carelessly, one front wheel on the pavement. 'That's yours, is it?'

'If only,' said Charles. 'We're in Sarah's Golf.' He didn't mention his Bristol garaged in Westminster. He chanced another small flare. 'You like deep blue, do you?'

There was a flicker of watchfulness in James's eye, a fractional hesitation. Because he was looking for it, Charles feared he might have imagined it. But he was fairly sure. 'I don't like cars of any colour,' said James. 'Never have.'

They didn't speak until they were approaching the M40. Sarah was driving. 'One word,' said Charles, 'for the evening, what would it be?'

'Brittle.'

'Good word.'

'She went through the motions with me but she couldn't get enough of you, could she? Is she like that with all men?'

'Reputedly.'

'She's trouble, that one. I'd steer well clear if I were you. He's not exactly a bundle of fun, either.'

'I think he's up to something. There's something going on.'

'What?'

'Not sure yet.'

'Wasted evening, then.'

'Not entirely.'

On the Sunday morning, they were sitting with their coffees on the terrace overlooking the Windrush, grey and sluggish that day, when Robin Cleveley rang.

'Have you seen the *Sunday Times*? ... Well, you should. You're all over it, both of you. Page four, with a taster on the front page. Whitehall's most famous spy coupling, the woman behind successive Chiefs of MI6, an unofficial legal resource for MI6 black operations, coincidental death of disgraced predecessor of Charles Thoroughgood, lack of a knighthood for Thoroughgood continues to puzzle observers. Bylined *Sunday Times* reporters. Any ideas?'

They walked into Burford and read the story over a bar lunch in the Lamb. Sarah was more surprised and upset than Charles, whose expectations of humanity were generally lower. 'How could they? All this personal stuff about how we got together, which we'd only told them because they asked, it's outrageous. And all this pure invention about my job. God knows what they're going to say about it in the office, they hate this kind of publicity. So will some of my clients. As for the implication that there was anything mysterious about Matthew's death and that we might have been somehow responsible for it – well, it's not quite actionable but I wish it were. God, I'm inclined to ring that woman and give her a piece of my mind. As for a return match, she can forget that.'

'It was probably Jam rather than her. He has form for this sort of thing. Although they've dressed it up as new there's actually nothing there that hasn't been in the media already.'

'She was complicit. She will have known he was doing it. And isn't it damaging for you? What will people at work think?'

'They expect this sort of thing.'

As they picked their way back through the cow-patted meadows, she said, 'And what about this knighthood business? Is that another invention? Matthew didn't have one.'

'He hadn't been in post long enough. Neither have I. No one gets one on appointment. We're on the Foreign Office list and it usually comes when you're about halfway through. In MI5, they're on the Home Office list and it usually comes along when they leave. Though the last two have peerages, not sure why. Probably because there haven't been any recent bombs in London.'

'Will this mean you're less likely to get it? Not that I dream of being Lady Thoroughgood. Sounds like some bewigged trollop in a Restoration comedy.'

'No idea. They're trying to cut down on automatic honours, anyway.' He regarded the honours system as harmless, benign and usefully cost-effective. But it wasn't that part of the story he was thinking about. It was a paragraph alleging past episodes of MI6 'unseen and unaccountable' manipulation of the law through sympathetic lawyers to stymie legitimate protest and frustrate international links between concerned groups. It cited incidents in the Cold War when student leaders and other radicals were arrested and accused of minor criminal offences in order to silence protest, implying that Charles had been involved and that his marriage to Sarah meant he still was. It was largely untrue but there was a germ of truth that few apart from James could know about.

'I suppose we'll never be free of this, our back story,' she remarked later. 'In one version or another. It's got everything, hasn't it? Young love, a love triangle, rejection, ambition, career rivals, betrayal, love renewed, sudden death convenient to career advantage followed by marriage made in heaven. The only thing missing is

Martin, which is just as well. They'd have a field day with him.'

Their adopted son – their dead son – was rarely mentioned between them, though he remained a presence. 'The past is the price we pay for the present,' said Charles. 'We wouldn't be here if it weren't for that.'

'Very profound, m'lud.'

Chapter Eleven

The Present

During the drive back to London that night he resumed his mental reassembly of those periods of his own past featuring Deep Blue. It was best done chronologically; otherwise, uncorrected by context, scenes and incidents could warp narrative.

The 1980s

He had reported to Hookey after his meeting with Federov, then written up the encounter in Hookey's outer office – which, for the time being, was as far as the report would travel. The following day he had resumed his desk in the EC liaison section.

'Broke my personal best while you were away,' said Mike. 'Four minutes thirty. Would have been better if the cleaners hadn't moved the waste bin, which meant I had to stretch right across from my safe to yours. Harold was muttering about that EC threat-warning strategy paper again. If you don't crack on with it I'll get lumbered and I'm going on leave. God knows how Freddie Farquarson managed three fifty-nine.'

'Harold said there was no hurry about the paper when I spoke to him last week.'

'There wasn't then. But if we don't get something in we won't get invited to the next lux freebie. Doesn't matter what's in the paper because no one pays any attention and MI5 are bound to do some earnest bit of work anyway. Pity we can't crib from theirs.'

'I wonder if we could.' Charles was thinking of Sue, whom he would see the next day when the tech-op was due to go into the Melburys' flat. 'I'll see if we can borrow it. Where is Harold?'

'Liaising.'

Harold drifted in some time after lunch. Charles popped his head round the door. 'Ah, the secret squirrel returns,' Harold said, as if he had been at his own desk all the time. 'Master Race let you go at last?' The Master Race was what people sometimes called the Sovbloc controllerate, not always affectionately. Harold held up his hand before Charles could reply. 'It's all right, don't tell me. Not prying. Need to know.'

'I was wondering about this EC threat-warning strategy paper.'

'Have you finished it?'

'Not quite. I thought—'

'Freddie – Freddie Farquarson, before your time, wonderful chap, very good officer – got away two years running with submitting the same paper. Went on jollies to Geneva and Vienna on the strength of it. You could dust his off and use it. So long as you change the date, which he forgot to do, second time.'

'I was wondering about cribbing the MI5 one if I can get hold of a draft.'

'Splendid idea. Highest tradition of the Service. By the way, have you heard who's going to be our new master, the new C/Europe? Angus Copplestone, your recent boss. Ambitious chap, isn't he? Bit of a shit?'

'He won't be pleased to find me here.'

Harold leaned back with his hands behind his head, gazing out over south London. 'When I joined ambition was a dirty word, second worst thing you could say about anyone after disloyalty. What people said about Philby. Shouldn't worry about Copplestone, though. Bosses come and go. Just make yourself scarce. That's what I do.'

The two-man MI5 team arrived at Charles's flat the following afternoon, carrying toolbags and looking like the electricians they essentially were. Telecheck had shown that the Melburys had booked themselves on a train to Glasgow.

'Sue's coming later with the CEs,' they said, unpacking an array of tools and drills. 'Clandestine entry team. They're having a butcher's in the flat. Give us a chance to confirm we're getting it right, too. What's all these wires in this cupboard?'

'New HT leads for my car. I haven't fitted them yet.'

Discussion of Charles's car occupied them until Sue arrived, slightly breathless from having hurried up the stairs. 'The CEs are in now. Downstairs.'

'How?' asked Charles.

'Lock-picking. They're good at that. Domestic targets like this take about thirty seconds.'

'What if the Turnips return unexpectedly?'

'We'd get plenty of notice. There's an SV team with them on the Glasgow train.'

'Late bath for them, then,' said one of the team.

'Bags over overtime, though.' She turned to Charles. 'D'you want a quick look when they've finished searching and before they lock up?'

By the time they went down about half an hour later, the team had drilled through Charles's floor in two places, one above the Melburys' sitting room and the other above the hall. They inserted diminutive probe microphones and connected them to recording equipment in his bedroom wardrobe. 'Dump your running kit, HT leads and any other clobber on top of it,' they said. 'If your girlfriend asks about it tell her it's an old answerphone system you've hung on to in case the new one packs up. It's designed to look like that. Except you haven't got a new one, have you?'

'No. Nor a girlfriend, any more.'

'Nothing to do with us, I hope?' asked Sue.

'Not fundamentally.'

'What's that supposed to mean?'

'Tell you later.'

The CE team comprised a man and a woman. Everyone talked in whispers. 'Nothing of obvious interest,' said the man, 'except a client list and purchase and sales records, which we've copied.' He nodded at the document-copying camera and small tripod held by the woman. 'There's some keys we can't identify – nothing to do with the flat – so we've copied them. But we can't do a proper job on the place unless we go through all these books, which would take about a month.'

'No sign of SW stuff or messed-about-with radios?' asked Sue.

The man shook his head. 'Nothing that could be used for secret writing unless they've got a method we don't know about. Radio and TV normal. Lots of Ordnance Survey maps, though, different parts of the country. Got a list of their numbers, nothing marked on them. Nothing handwritten anywhere, no notes, scraps, lists, nothing. Very tidy couple.'

The woman led them through to the kitchen, where the telephone was in pieces on the table. 'This is why we didn't need a mike in here,' she said, holding up a piece of the dismantled receiver. 'This is now our mike. Picks up anything in this room and sends it straight back down the line to us.'

Sue came back to his flat while the team finished off and left.

'Supposing someone had caught us down there today and called the police?' he asked. 'Are you legally covered?'

'Home Sec warrant. Signed by himself. We have to for break-ins. May I have a look outside?'

He opened the French windows on to the small balcony at the back, overlooking private gardens surrounded on four sides by nineteenth-century red-brick apartment buildings. From his top-floor balcony, they looked straight into the tops of plane trees.

'Wonderful. You're so lucky.'

'Where do you live?'

'Balham.'

'Could be worse.'

'Yeah. Could be more Balham.'

He was tempted to ask whether alone or with anyone but instead told her about the EC threat assessment paper. 'If whoever's doing it in your service could let me see a draft, just to make sure we don't conflict . . .'

She laughed. 'So you can copy it, you mean? Top and tail it, insert MI6 for MI5?'

'I might add a few words of my own.'

'God, you live up to your reputation, you lot. Or down to it. All right, I'll ask our liaison people to wing a draft over to you. I suppose the Brits need to present a united front. In return, you can tell me what's happened with your girlfriend. Haven't pushed her off this balcony, have you?'

He explained as succinctly as he could while they stood sipping tea and gazing into the treetops.

'That's quite funny, really,' she said. 'But not for her. You don't sound exactly heartbroken.'

'I wonder if I should get back in touch and try to explain more.'

'I'd leave it if I were you, if you're not really interested. Don't raise her hopes again. Mind if I use your phone to ring the Office?'

He washed and dried the mugs.

She put the phone down. 'They've lost them. The Turnips.'

'On a train? How?'

'When they got off, stupid. They went to the nearest car-hire place in Glasgow and hired a car. The team – there were only two of them, pretending to be a couple – couldn't hire their own in time to follow them. They've got the car details and we'll have to get Security Branch to get details from the hire company. They're on the train back now. The team, that is.'

'Fancy a drink, pizza or anything?'

'Another time. I've got to go. But thanks.' She stopped. 'Really, another time.'

A week or so later, Charles recalled, he was sent to France again. They had heard from the heart surgeon that Federov had made an appointment, tagging it on to another trip to Paris.

'Either it illustrates that he's right about his ability to fix things,' said Hookey, 'or it's evidence for Security Branch suspicions that he's being played against us. Trouble with so many of these cases is that, in the early stages particularly, almost everything can be argued either way.' He laid the tip of his middle finger on the handwritten pink memo on his desk, the only paper there apart from the Green Book, the Diplomatic Service list. 'The Russians are tying up this engine deal with the French. He was right about that, anyway – they're not buying Rolls-Royce engines. You must see him in France, not here. He must be squeaky clean while he's here. Get your access agent to set up something for you and ideally then get him out of the way. This time you must get more to satisfy the doubters. It's a big thing, what we're doing for him, and it's a big risk he's taking. We need him to tell us something important, verifiable and new. Ideally, something on which we can act.'

'Should I warn Angus – H/Paris – in case I run into him again? I got away with it last time, but only just.'

'Of course, H/Paris, our new Controller Europe-in-waiting.' Hookey smiled at some thought he wasn't sharing. 'I'll have a word with his about-to-be predecessor, the current C/Europe, let him know we're poaching, but not what.' He spun the memo round with his finger. 'Meanwhile, I hear your neighbours are up to something in Scotland. Enough to get MI5 excited, anyway.'

'I know they went but haven't heard what for. The tech-op's working, anyway.'

'Get over and see them this morning. Say I've asked for you to be briefed. Harold can spare you, I daresay.'

*

'Sorry,' said Sue, 'I've been on leave. Someone should have briefed you, in outline anyway; although, strictly speaking, you don't need to know.'

Charles shrugged to show he didn't mind. 'So long as we can have that pizza.'

'Today, now? Right. Let me fill you in before we go.' She pushed her hair back behind her ears and leaned forward, elbows on the desk. Telecheck had confirmed that the Melburys had returned two nights after eluding surveillance in Glasgow. Special Branch had established from the hire company that they had travelled 270 miles in their hired Ford Fiesta and that the sole driver was Mr Melbury, who had shown a British driving licence with his London address. The company had a record of its number.

'Like to know how he got that so quickly and whether it's real,' Sue said. 'We're checking with Swansea.'

They had paid by credit card from their business account, saying they were spending a couple of days sightseeing in the Highlands. Further SB enquiries had shown they had spent one night in a hotel in Faslane and had driven round to Coulport.

'It could of course just be coincidental that Faslane is where our nuclear subs are based,' said Sue, 'and that Coulport on Loch Long is where the nuclear warheads are stored and loaded. But an interesting coincidence.'

'Why would they want to go there, what could they learn? Satellites can surely do all the reconnaissance.'

'Meeting someone? Clearing or filling another DLB? Birdwatching? Let's have that pizza.'

Charles was back in Century House when Josef rang. He was excited and it was impossible to get him to be discreet on the phone. 'It is done. We meet for drink. Already I have room in same hotel.'

Charles recalled the previous bill. 'That's not necessary. You can visit him there or arrange to meet somewhere else.'

'It is booked. He wishes me to be there so he comes to my room at night when others are sleeping. He telephone me and say please be there. It is open between us, you see, that I know what he is doing. And it is better for you because you can see him when he come to me.'

'OK.' There was nothing to be done now. A way of doing it without Josef would have to be found for future meetings.

'Yvette, she does not come. The drinking is not good for her, I tell her. Only I come.'

Charles was in Paris two days later, travelling by the Newhaven-Dieppe ferry rather than fly and risk Russian monitoring of airline passenger lists which could – conceivably – show that wherever Federov travelled, so did someone they knew or believed to be a British MI6 officer. This was largely to mollify Security Branch, who had wanted him to travel under alias until he pointed out that he had worked with the French security service in his own name. He might still – just – get away with saying he was there to visit his girlfriend.

'And what if they ask who she is or want to interview her?'

'A married lady, wife of a colleague. I refuse to compromise her.' A greater secret could often be hidden beneath a lesser. 'Or I could actually take someone, someone conscious and trustworthy. In fact, I know a woman in—'

'Dirty weekend in Paris at taxpayer's expense, eh, Charles? Nice work if you can get it.'

He booked into a modest tourist hotel in Montmartre, remaining in the small green room with its small mirror, small bed and small framed photograph of Notre Dame only as long as it took to unpack. He always found small hotel rooms depressing, as if all life, all hopes and strivings, had come down to this. Places in which to die obscurely, not to live. He spent the afternoon in a café, reading an Iris Murdoch novel and watching the street life, keeping clear of central Paris in case he ran into anyone from the embassy.

At six-thirty he strode with assumed confidence through the foyer of the George V, carrying the Murdoch in which were folded a couple of blank sheets of A4. He preferred note-taking to recording. He reached the lifts unchallenged.

There was no answer to his knock on Josef's fifth-floor door. He knocked again, waited, listened for voices and reluctantly concluded he'd have to check the room number with reception. Then the lift opened to reveal Josef wearing a brown leather jacket and a white baseball cap. He was smiling and his tie was askew. 'Mr Thoroughgood, I come for you. I am with him. We wait for you. Now you come.'

Charles held the door open and checked there was no one else in the corridor. 'We agreed your room. Why are you in his?'

'I wait for him. He does not come. So I go to him. It is OK. He had delay. We go to him now. He is expecting.' He swayed slightly.

A door along the corridor opened. Charles stepped into the lift. 'Which floor?'

Federov's room was a suite, smelling of drink. A black overcoat lay on the floor behind the sofa, there was a half-full bottle of vodka and two empty wine bottles on the coffee table and a glass on its side beneath. Fedorov, wearing suit and tie, stood by the desk. Josef went straight to the fridge and took out a bottle of champagne.

Charles addressed Federov. 'This is not a good time or place. We could be interrupted. You go to London tomorrow?'

Federov nodded very slightly. His dark eyes were doleful. He's as plastered as Josef, Charles thought. Josef said something in Russian and Federov pointed to the glass on the floor. Josef missed a step and almost fell as he went to pick it up.

'We can't talk now, like this,' said Charles. 'I'll see you in London, but only if we can do it safely. You still have the number I gave you?' Federov nodded again. 'Ring me from your hotel. We must talk.'

There was a groan, a thump and a crash from behind. The champagne bottle rolled across the carpet, unopened. The coffee table was upended and Josef lay on his side between it and the sofa. Charles moved the table and bent down to him.

'He is drunk,' said Federov.

He was, but there was something else. He lay on his side, eyes and mouth open, lips and cheeks tinged blue. 'I think he's had a heart attack,' said Charles.

Federov moved for the first time, pushing the table aside and kneeling alongside Charles. At first they both hesitated to touch him, then Charles – unsure whether he was doing right – carefully pushed Josef's uppermost shoulder so that he lay on his back. Federov lifted the leg that was crossed over the other and they pushed the sofa back out of the way. Charles felt vainly for a pulse in both wrists and then – because he had seen it in films – in the side of the neck. Then he felt Josef's chest for a heartbeat.

'Should we try mouth-to-mouth?' He still half hoped that Federov might know what to do.

'Mouth?' Federov looked puzzled.

Charles had practised on a dummy a couple of years

before during an office first-aid demonstration of what was then thought to be the best technique, but wasn't sure he remembered what to do. 'You push on his chest,' he said, indicating with both hands. 'I'll do mouth-to-mouth.' He didn't relish it and it took surprising effort to get Josef's heavy head in the right position, then some fiddling to pull his tongue flat while all the time his arm was jogged by Federov's energetic pushing on Josef's chest. He could taste alcohol on Josef's lips.

After a minute or two they both stopped. Federov was flushed and panting. Charles remembered it was he who was supposed to have the heart condition. Explaining one body would be bad enough. 'Can you feel anything?'

'He is dead.' They stared, each seeing the same thought reflected in the other's eye, the same shameful absence of concern for Josef himself. Their thoughts were all of consequences. 'It must not be here,' said Federov. 'He cannot die here. There would be questions, we could not explain.'

Charles imagined police, an inquest, delay, publicity, questioning of Federov, questioning of himself, breaking it to Yvette. 'We've got to move him, get him back to his room.'

'How?'

'Carry him. I'll carry him, I'll pretend he's drunk. If you help me lift him.'

It was easier said than done. Josef was thickset anyway and had put on weight in later life. Charles took him by the shoulders, keeping the head upright against his own stomach, while Federov took the feet. The body sagged so much in the middle that it was difficult to lift it high enough to get it on to the sofa. Federov was panting again.

'Rest,' said Charles.

Federov sat on the arm of the sofa, his face haggard. 'Too heavy,' he said. 'I cannot.'

'I'll do it. Fireman's lift.' He had to explain that. 'If anyone sees me I'll say he's drunk.'

'You take the lift? It is two floors.'

'Stairs. Less chance of being seen.'

There was a glint of humour in Federov's tired, dark eyes. 'You are weightlifter?'

'Only for tonight.'

They both looked at Josef. 'He would laugh,' said Federov.

'He would.'

He had to kneel on the floor before the sofa to get Josef across his shoulders, then use his quadriceps to lift. He hadn't carried anyone like this since he was in the army when they had to race each other, but then you were paired with someone roughly your own size and weight. Josef felt like two men and his head lolled heavily against Charles's back.

Federov opened the door slightly, then closed it. 'People at lift.'

Charles, stooped and staring at the carpet, nodded. He didn't want to waste breath on words. Only when

ALAN JUDD

he felt Federov's touch on the back of his right hand, the one hooked around Josef's thigh, did he look up.

'Mr Thoroughgood.' Federov paused until Charles was looking directly at him. 'I thank you for this. I will not forget.'

Charles nodded again. It was an effort to hold up his head.

Federov opened the door, looked out, opened it wider and stood back. As Charles stepped through, he spoke again: 'Deep Blue.'

Trying to manoeuvre Josef through the door, Charles could barely turn his head.

'There is KGB plan to take it,' said Federov. 'They will put it somewhere and make confusion to kill and frighten people. Go now.' He shut the door.

By the time Charles reached the stairs at the end of the corridor he badly wanted to rest, but if he put Josef down he doubted he'd get him up again. The effort made him less deferential of his burden; he opened one of the double doors to the stairs with Josef's feet and felt the head knock against the other as he turned. Two floors up meant four flights of stairs. His pauses between them lengthened as his thighs weakened. He stood bent and panting before the last flight, muscles quivering in his thighs and his knees threatening to buckle. He had done this and more in the army, not so very many years before, and felt no older now than then. But if anyone had appeared he wouldn't have had the breath to explain.

Only when he reached the room door did he realise that the key must be in Josef's pocket. It was impossible to search him without putting him down. He knelt as slowly as he could but lost control, so that Josef slipped from his shoulders with a prolonged crumple, his head banging against the doorpost. Charles tried to keep the body propped up in a sitting position but it slumped to the side. No one who saw it would now believe it was a drunk.

Searching Josef's pockets felt almost as intimate as the failed kiss of life. The keys were in his left trouser pocket, difficult to retrieve because they were attached to a piece of polished wood. When he opened the door Josef fell in. He stepped across the body and tried to drag it in by the shoulders but it was too heavy for his weakened state. He took the still-warm hands and pulled it across the thick carpet, inches at a time. As he closed the door he heard the lift and voices in the corridor. He leaned against the wall, panting and sweating.

Chapter Twelve

The 1980s

'So the hotel called the police, not you?'

'I just called reception, told them he seemed to have had a heart attack and asked for an ambulance. I couldn't just leave him because his wife would know he was meeting me and it would look suspicious if I scarpered. Then the whole story might have come out. But I didn't mention the police.'

'But they arrived first and started quizzing you, who you were, what you were doing in the room, that sort of thing, and you said you were having a drinking session with your old friend when he just keeled over?'

'I'd emptied a bottle and a half from his bar down the sink and taken a swig or two to make sure I smelled of it. Also messed up the room a bit.'

'And all went well until one of them asked what he was doing taking an expensive room like that when he lived not far away and you said it was to meet you and maybe other friends and they thought that was a tad unlikely and started enquiring more deeply?'

'Yes.'

'Not surprised. And then the next day the shit hit the fan.' Hookey tapped the copy of *Le Monde* on his desk, open at the page showing a small photograph of Charles over a story headlined, BRITISH DIPLOMAT IN HOTEL DEATH FRACAS.

'Presumably leaked by the police or someone in the hotel,' said Charles.

'Obviously.' Hookey's tone was as dry as sandpaper.

Although recounting the experience was nothing like as bad as living through it, Hookey's cool questioning again made Charles feel the inadequacy of his off-the-cuff cover story. Had the ambulance arrived sooner the police might not have lingered and then strayed beyond taking Josef's details to Charles himself – why were they meeting here, was it really for nothing more than a drinking session, where was he staying, had he come to Paris just for this, what was his job? Instinct and training persuaded Charles to stick to his story about keeping in touch with an old friend of whom he was fond; however unlikely, it couldn't be proved wrong. As for the rest, checkable truths were the best answer; Angus Copplestone or the ambassador could vouch for him at the embassy. Reluctantly persuaded, the police nonetheless took away his passport and would not allow him back to his hotel until he had made a statement at the police station. He was not under arrest – quite – but was under investigation and not to leave Paris until the cause of death had been satisfactorily established. Once allowed back to his hotel, he worried less about the French judicial system, with its assumption of guilt, than the reactions of the embassy and the Foreign Office. He rang Yvette to find her tearful and incoherent, having already heard from the police. They had also questioned her about Charles. There was no question of ringing Hookey on an open international line.

'So the next morning you pitched up at the embassy at sparrow's fart and Angus Copplestone let you into the station to send your de-you telegram to me,' said Hookey.

'Not exactly. The station wasn't open but Alex, the head secretary, arrived first and opened up the comms for me.'

'Which rubbed salt into Angus's wound, finding you communicating with Head Office on a case on his patch he not only didn't know about but couldn't even find out about because a decipher-yourself telegram leaves no record in the station. Then he had to say nice things about you to the French police and then confess all to the ambassador.'

'And all because I'd disobeyed him by not terminating an agent.'

'Terminated instead by the Almighty.' Hookey swivelled his chair to gaze out of the window. 'Then the press coverage. More salt for Angus.'

'Just the one article.'

'So far. As it is, sufficient for the Chief to be summoned by the Permanent Under-Secretary to explain to the Foreign Office. And for Angus to make a formal complaint to me via his controller. All this on top of our already having to seek retrospective clearance for your offer of defector status to a senior Russian official. What you might call a first-class bloody cock-up, don't you think?'

Charles nodded his acknowledgement, though he couldn't help feeling it was slightly unfair: agents didn't usually die in meetings. But he was inhibited from defending himself by the obvious inadequacy of his cover story; he should have gone prepared with a better one. Reputations in MI6, for good or ill, were easily won and hard to lose. This wasn't going to do much for his. Hookey's laugh, abrupt as a bark, startled him.

Hookey swivelled away from the window, grinning. 'Cock-ups always give pleasure, schadenfreude all round, that's why everyone loves them. Except whoever has to carry the can, of course. Important thing is that you kept our friend Badger – that's his code-name now, by the way, he's got one now – out of it. A case-saving – perhaps for him a life-saving – effort. You did the right thing. Well done.'

Surprised by a wave of relief, Charles realised he had been more worried than he had acknowledged to himself.

'Let's hope he'll show his appreciation long-term,'

Hookey continued. 'Now that you've made it possible there still is a long-term. That cryptic remark he made about blue something – what was it?'

'Deep Blue. He said, "The KGB have a plan. They will put it somewhere and make confusion to kill and frighten people."'

'Doesn't get us very far, does it? Sounds more like a pop group. Maybe some new weapon we've got, missile system. There was one called Blue Streak but that got dumped years ago. Something they think they can pinch, obviously. You should tell MI5 about it. They want to see you, anyway. Left a message.'

'So it's OK to tell them about Badger?'

'Not at all. Say it's in a report from one of our Sovbloc cases you know nothing about, that I told you because we'll report it in writing to them in due course. I'm dining with Director K tonight, anyway. I'll sort it out with him.' He stood and took his coat from the wooden hat-stand. 'Great pity you were detained in Paris while Badger was here. According to the sawbones, the operation is do-able, he's given Badger some pills and will let us know as soon as they sort out a date. That'll make two mighty big favours Badger owes us. Just hope you'll get a chance to see him again and find out about that blue thing.'

'Fancy a coffee?' Sue stood and hitched her bag over her shoulder. 'Let's go out.' She turned to the two women who shared her office. 'Anyone want anything?'

Neither did. 'Daft having to leave an MI5 office in order to talk about something confidential,' she said as they descended the Gower Street stairs. 'Maggie does Poles and Ruth does Czechs and they really shouldn't overhear anything about Russian Illegals. Not that there's normally much to hear. Anyway, I needed to stretch my legs. If I spend all day in the office I feel groggy by the end.'

'I know what you mean.'

'Don't see how, you're never there. I've never once rung Century House and got you. You do really work there, don't you?'

'I go there most days, if that's what you mean.'

They crossed the Euston Road to a backstreet café where background noise and table separation were about right. He told her about the Deep Blue warning. It meant nothing to her but she promised to report it and get back to him. Then she leaned across the table and lowered her voice. 'Your recent ex, the one you were telling me about, did you say her name was Micklethwaite, Janet Micklethwaite? With a brother in Hartlepool?'

'I don't know. She has two brothers, one a geologist in Canada whom I've never met and one a semi-dropout. Dropped out of university, trained as a teacher, dropped out of teaching and lived in some sort of commune, became very political, then went back to teaching, supply teaching, last I heard. Family was pleased about it, I remember Janet saying.'

'Called James? And did she say where he's working?'

'Called Jim at home, Jam to his friends. Teaching somewhere, not sure where.'

Sue sat back and looked seriously at him, as if assessing him for a job or trying to decide whether he could be trusted with a loan. She was not beautiful, he thought, nor pretty like Janet, but her features were clear and regular and her straightforwardness and energy appealing. 'You know him, anyway?' she asked.

'Not well; we met a few times when he came down here to stay with her or see his parents. Aggressively left-wing and pleased with himself. Probably thought the same of me, apart from the left-wing bit.'

'So you don't know him well enough to get in touch with him? Would you be prepared to get in touch with her again?'

'Last time you were saying I shouldn't. You're going to have to tell me more.'

'Three nights ago Mr Turnip went out by himself and made a call from a callbox. We know this because the tech-op picked up her saying, "Isn't it time you made the call?" and him saying, "Another thirty minutes." Then she says, "You won't use the one round the corner?" and he says, "No, the King's Road one, the one we used before." We worked out he meant not the one nearest your flat but the pair on the King's Road going back towards Sloane Square, so we did a check on the numbers dialled from those two. One was out of order, surprise, surprise, but the other showed a call to Hartlepool at about the time he would have got to the callbox. There was also another call to the same number exactly a week before. The number is registered to James Anthony Micklethwaite. It's an unusual name and I suddenly remembered what you'd said about Janet. Huge coincidence, if it really is him.'

'So you want me to find out about him through Janet?'

'Well, what he's up to, where he works and what-ever. I mean, we can get a lot through the social security computer in Newcastle but she might know stuff that's not recorded. Quite understand if you don't want to get in touch with her, of course.'

'But for Queen and country, I suppose?'

'Not asking you to ... you know ... resume the relationship again. Just, if you can have a chat for old times' sake, as it were. Although it's a bit soon for that, I admit.'

They talked office gossip over two more coffees. As they were leaving, she said, 'You will do it, then?'

'Don't give up, do you?'

She smiled. 'Not when I want something.'

He met Janet a few nights later in a sawdust-and-wine bar in Battersea called Angela's and Peter's, neutral territory. Ringing to set it up had not been easy.

'What's the point, what is there to say?' she had asked.

'I know, I know, it's just that – well, it would be

nice to be on friendly terms. No need for a Cold War. Jaw-jaw better than war-war.' It was not the first time he had manipulated his private life in the interests of the professional but repetition didn't make it easier.

As it turned out, there were no arguments or silences, with both talking energetically about anything but themselves. Her asking after his mother and sister made it natural for him to ask about her family.

'And Jimmy, what's he up to now?'

She sighed and looked at the sawdust as if to discern some pattern in James's life. 'Well, he's working again, anyway, in a comprehensive in County Durham. God knows how, it's meant to be quite a good school. He's even renting a house rather than squatting. Rejoining bourgeois society, though no one dare say that, of course.'

'Maybe there's a good woman behind him.'

'We'd be the last to know. He lives alone. Mother went to see him. She said the flat was reasonably tidy, almost decent. No sign of a feminine hand.' She smiled. 'Like your flat.'

He sensed a resumption would be possible, that perhaps she wanted it, which made him feel worse. 'No sign of Swiss Roll, then?'

Swiss Roll was the family nickname for a woman James had brought home whose dietary principles prevented her from eating anything Janet's mother produced except some Swiss rolls forgotten in a cake tin. She had come only once.

'She went back to Greenham Common, where he found her. You know, that all-women anti-nuclear protest camp in Berkshire.'

'I didn't know he was involved with that.'

'I don't know how much he was. He hung around it, anyway. All his friends were on protests of one sort or another. I could never understand what they lived off.'

'Us, I guess.' It was an incautious remark, a reminder of their disagreements about the welfare state. Janet was fond of her brother, despite disagreeing with him, and it was dangerous to link the two subjects. 'Good luck to them,' he added, insincerely.

'Actually, he mentioned you last time I spoke to him. He's still got a book of yours that I lent him, the one by that Austrian about an army officer who gets married or something.'

'*Beware of Pity*. Great novel by—'

'I never read it. Don't suppose he has. But it's a hard-back, first edition in English. Quite old.'

'Well, I could drop in and pick it up. I've got to go to North Yorkshire, not far from County Durham. Supposed to be learning about radar installations.' He plucked that out of the air, confident he could cite the early-warning station at Fylingdales if pressed. He had glimpsed it through swirling snow on an army escape and evasion exercise on the moors, huge golf balls clustered on a hilltop. It had been so cold that most escapees had longed for capture, regardless of the indignities of interrogation.

Janet opened her handbag. 'I have his number here.'

'Sorry to dump this on you,' Mike said cheerfully the following morning. 'But I'm off on leave tonight. Got so much left from my posting that I've got to use it or lose it. Harold said he would help you out if he could but he can't because he's busy.'

'With what?'

'Liaising. You must admit you've had it pretty easy since you got here, always off on some Master Race jaunt or something.'

Charles couldn't deny that. He had come to regard his sojourns in EC Liaison as rest periods during which making a few changes to the MI5 draft of the Security Liaison Policy paper Sue had sent over counted as work. But the pleasant monotony had been spoiled this morning by Mike's revelation that he was expected to shepherd a Greek liaison visit around the UK.

'Programme's already mapped out by the head of station, H/Athens. He can't be here himself to do it, more's the pity. All you have do is bear-lead them for four days, day and a night here in London, day and a night down at the Castle, day and a night up North visiting a power station in County Durham.'

'Why a power station?'

'Nuclear power station, security of. They want to know how we protect them. This one's in Hartlepool, one of the more hospitable ones, apparently. Keen to show people round. FCO often use it.'

The coincidence was useful, given what Sue had asked him to do, but he didn't want his visit to James to be tied to a liaison visit. 'Surely MI5—'

'Tried that. They're full up with liaison-and-training visits, which is what they always say. Ditto MOD.'

'The Foreign Office . . . ?'

'Greeks won't wear it. They want us. H/Athens is very keen for us to push the boat out because he'll get better results from liaison. There's only three of them, a bloke from military security and a man and woman from their MI5 equivalent. It'll be a cinch. All you have to do is open doors and eat and drink and be nice. Telegrams are all here somewhere.' He gathered up a pile of telegrams and dumped them in Charles's in-tray. 'Makes sense for you to have everything as I'm away from tonight. Greek ones are in there somewhere. I'll tell the girls to bring everything to you whether you're copied on it or not so you don't miss anything. Ask them what to do if you don't know anything. Better than waiting for Harold.'

'Where is Harold?'

'Liaising. What he always does. Between ourselves, I think he liaises in detail with a woman from the Italian Embassy. Nice work if you can get it.'

It was hard to imagine Harold liaising energetically, but perhaps that was where his energy went. 'When does Angus Copplestone become our new controller?'

'Tomorrow. Good luck.'

Charles's phone rang. 'Got a moment?'

Charles hurried up to the twelfth floor, to find Hookey's door closed. 'On the phone,' said Maureen. They talked until the light on her own phone went off but she still made no move. Charles heard a security cupboard door close and the spinning of the combination lock. 'Just putting his papers away,' she said.

'Has he always been this security-conscious?'

'He shared an office with George Blake at one time.' She went to Hookey's door, opened it a little to check, then opened it wide for Charles. 'Tea or coffee?'

'He won't have time,' Hookey called out.

He didn't wait for Charles to sit. 'I've briefed Director K on Badger. He'll now be formally indoctrinated. And we discussed this other case of theirs you're helping with, the two Illegals. Suspected Illegals. They don't know what they're up to and don't have enough on them to have them arrested but they're pretty sure they're not what they're pretending to be. Nor do they have the resources to keep them under surveillance indefinitely. I understand the Illegals have made clandestine contact with someone connected with you – girlfriend's brother or something? – and want you to go and sniff him out. Meanwhile, Badger's heart man now tells me he could summon him over for his op any day, provided he can get out of Moscow, so we want you to be permanently on call to get alongside him and ask him about this Deep Blue thing before he

149

goes under the knife. Last thing we want is for him to snuff it without telling us. We'll get notice that he's travelling when he applies for his visa, but not much, which means you've got to be instantly available. OK?'

'So MI5 know all about—'

'Director K does, your desk officer doesn't. No need to know.'

'And Director K doesn't know what—'

'He's checking all UK, US and NATO systems and projects but no Deep Blues have come up yet. You'll be the first to know if it does. I've got a meeting now. Any questions?'

Charles told him about the Greek liaison visit.

Hookey shrugged. 'Well, you'll just have to dump them if it happens. Leave them at the Castle. They can look after them.'

'I'd better square it with Angus Copplestone, who takes over tomorrow. What can I tell him about—'

Hookey's secretary put her head round the door. 'They're here.'

Hookey stood. 'Nothing. Don't tell him anything. Cross that bridge when you come to it. Refer him to me.'

Chapter Thirteen

The Present

'Elspeth is not ...' Robin Cleveley sighed and shook his head. Like Melanie Stokes, he too-obviously relished the intimacy implied by using a minister's first name. 'Elspeth is not best pleased.' They were sitting over coffee in Charles's club, in corner chairs in the morning room. 'But I've reassured her that you weren't deliberately seeking publicity because you resented not having been knighted. I told a white lie – I said you weren't bothered about getting a K, or anything else.'

'It wasn't a lie.'

Charles had described the origin of the *Sunday Times* story, swallowing his resentment at having to account to Robin for it rather than the Foreign Secretary herself. They had pulled at all the loose ends of the subject without untangling it.

'What I do get,' said Robin, 'is that, having got her dainty hands on MI5, Melanie wants to do down MI6 in the competition for head offices and resources.

She's going the wrong way about it, in my view, but the motive is at least comprehensible. What I don't get – given her closeness to the Home Secretary and her ambitions with regard to the governing party – is why she's shacked up with a far-left creep like Micklethwaite. Still less why she should participate in furthering his agenda, whatever it is. I mean, personally – from what you say – and certainly politically, they've got no more in common than ... well, you and him.'

Charles let that pass. They did indeed seem an unlikely pairing. 'Maybe it's one of those relationships that goes back a long way and is hard to get out of.'

'Hasn't stopped her playing around, though. With the Home Sec, for one. Before he became it. But it must be politically and socially awkward. If it was just a phase from early life you'd think she'd have moved on by now. Maybe he's got some kind of hold over her.'

'Hard to break relationship habits, sometimes.'

'Could she be a sleeper? I mean, not just a sleeper-around but, you know, worming her way into us in order to report back to James and his activist friends?'

'Then surely the last thing she'd do is parade her association with him.'

When eventually he stood to go, Robin looked proprietorially about him. 'I'm beginning to wonder about a club.'

Charles struggled with a suitable reaction. 'Have you looked at many others?'

'A few. I rather like Brooks's.'

'Good choice. Smart, very elegant. Worth considering.'

'But this place has its charms.'

'They all do in their different ways.' Some awkwardnesses, however awkward, could be turned to advantage. They walked slowly from the morning room. 'I've been meaning to say, you remember asking me if I knew anything about something called Deep Blue and all I could think of was the chess computer? What was that about?'

Robin shook his head. 'Wish I knew. It was a blog from one of your friend James's friends, a Triple A fanatic. Was SNP until he was expelled with a couple of like-minded cronies who were all for direct action: you know, burning English-owned houses, smashing shop windows, that sort of thing. He seems to have teamed up with James at about the time Triple A espoused nationalism – for Scotland, that is. So maybe we can expect a conflagration of second homes, bijou pads, manor houses and castles throughout the kingdom now.' He smiled.

They reached the steps outside. 'But what did he say about Deep Blue?'

'Nothing much. That was what was so interesting, given the reaction. We monitor these people on social media, know your enemy and all that. They tell you a lot about themselves. We all do, I'm afraid.' He surveyed Pall Mall from the top of the steps. 'World looks all right from here.'

'So what did he say?'

'Oh, it was just something like, "Good talk with Jam the other day about reviving Deep Blue, blast from the past. On your way, Trident." But you don't, do you? Do social media?'

'And what was the reaction?'

'Taken down the same day, disappeared. Elspeth was wondering whether you should, you know, raise the profile of MI6, sharpen the image. Start blogging yourself. C's blog. Get a lot of attention. I mean, if the Prime Minister can have one, why not C? That's her thinking.'

'She can think again. Tell her that from me.' Charles held out his hand. 'Who was he, this chap?'

'Calls himself "Rob's Ready" – Rob S. Ready. Don't know whether that's his real name. Is there a waiting list?'

'Probably. Might be quite long, dead men's shoes and all that.'

Robin grinned. 'Daresay you could arrange a few of those. Let me know.'

That afternoon in Croydon was largely taken up by a visit from the head of the Indian service, who was concerned less with matters of mutual interest than with warning about what his Pakistani opposite number was doing. Charles had hosted the Pakistani the week before and had been lectured on the iniquities of the Indian service. Each then went off to spend a few days at CIA headquarters in Langley. At the end of the afternoon he did what he had been tempted to do immediately after coffee with Robin but had resisted, more because he was usually suspicious of his own impulses than because he had thought better of it. He picked up his phone and dialled Melanie Stokes.

Her greeting was effusive even by her standards, which he interpreted as anxiety that he was going to attack her over the *Sunday Times* piece. He didn't mention it. 'A quick drink this evening,' he said. 'Possible?'

'Yes ... yes, that would be great.' She sounded relieved. 'Anything I—'

'Just a small matter of mutual interest. Won't take more than a glass. Maybe two.'

When he rang Sarah at work to tell her he would be late home, there was an uncharacteristic edge to her voice. 'You're seeing her? Why?'

'There's something she might know that I might be able to get out of her.'

'Don't go thinking you'll charm it out of her. She won't give anything away unless she's getting something.'

'I won't be on a charm expedition.'

'She will. Remember, I warned you about her.'

He was surprised; Sarah was not normally jealous of other women – or not so that she let show – and he thought it would have been obvious that

Melanie, spiky and clearly out to impress, was not what he found alluring. Not that he was looking to be allured, though he was always content to be charmed.

They met in the bar of a newish hotel behind MI5's Thames House headquarters. It was busy with young people whom he guessed were her staff. 'I should have suggested somewhere farther from your office,' he said, nodding at them.

She shook her head and, for the second time in about a minute, pushed back her hair. 'Doubt they're mine. This place is too expensive for them.'

It was tempting to take her up on her use of the possessive, since she had no executive authority at all, theoretically, but he let it pass.

'Any news on a new head office?' she asked.

'Gone quiet. Presumably being masticated somewhere in the bureaucratic maw.'

She did not pursue it. She would be doing all she could to undermine him but would see no point in further exposing her hand. She was waiting to hear what he wanted to discuss and probably still expected a row about the *Sunday Times* article. She pushed back her hair again.

He kept her waiting while the waitress brought their drinks. 'What do you want?' he asked.

'What do I want?'

Her surprise was genuine and he waited as she looked to see whether he was being playful or serious.

'In life. D'you want to be prime minister or the world's richest woman or founder of a dynasty or saviour of the world or what? Or none of the above?'

She smiled and relaxed. 'Or all of the above. I don't really know what I want. Except to be able to do whatever it is I want when I want. Do you? Do you know what you want? Or have you already got it?'

'I certainly never looked for this.' He smiled back. 'Wouldn't you like to be DG of MI5, though? Shape it and run it as you want rather than be a bird of passage, perched on the masthead?'

'I wouldn't want to be a bureaucrat. I'm no good at it, I just don't have the patience. Anyway, they wouldn't want me, I'd bring too much of the wrong kind of baggage.'

Charles raised his eyebrows.

'Political baggage. All my contacts. My adult life has been taken up with the political and you're not supposed to be political in the intelligence agencies, are you? Not actively political, anyway. And then there's personal baggage, a certain amount, anyway.'

'Drug dependency, gambling, alcohol addiction, mountain of debts and promiscuous intimacy with terrorists?' He guessed she would enjoy the attentiveness that came with teasing.

She smiled again, nodding and pushing her hair back. 'Plus, my living with a Triple A activist who's organising the Trafalgar Square peace protest.'

'But that's public-order business, isn't it, really?

Police business, as you were saying the other day? Nothing to concern MI5.'

'That's what I think, but there are those such as Michael Dunton who think some of what Triple A are doing constitutes subversion – you know, all that reds-under-the-beds Cold War stuff, spying on loyal trade unionists and all that. Fortunately, Michael's out of the way for the time being at least and Simon Mall just waits to be told what to think. Bears the imprint of the last person to sit on him. As for me, I think we need to keep well away from all that subversion stuff. And that's not just because of who I live with, though I guess James would be seen as baggage.'

Charles nodded, put down his glass and leaned forward, elbows on knees. 'Actually, it was terrorism, not subversion, I wanted to talk about.'

He didn't need to invent. Islamist terrorism was overwhelmingly MI5's main concern but also occupied a substantial and growing portion of MI6's effort and budget. There were always issues to be resolved, turf or territorial, ownership of cases, disagreements over tactics in joint cases. They were mostly sorted out at working level but were occasionally escalated to the boards of the two services. He rehearsed a couple of cases which he knew were on the point of resolution and which she wouldn't know about, seeking her agreement for what he knew would happen anyway.

She was intrigued and flattered. 'I don't normally get involved in operational discussions. Perhaps I should. The only way I hear about what's going on is if I ask.'

'We should keep in touch.'

When they stood to go, he said, 'Good to see James the other night. Trip down memory lane.'

'I wouldn't have thought you two had much in common.'

'We used to see a fair bit of each other.' It was an exaggeration. 'Hope he doesn't get into trouble with this Triple A stuff, this peace protest he's organising.'

'Plus, he raises money for the peace camp outside the nuclear submarine base at Faslane. He wants to make it as big as the women's camp at Greenham Common was. Ticks all the boxes, does James.' She was more relaxed now.

'Thinks we should ditch the deterrent, does he? No more Trident?'

'Ultimately, yes, but for the time being the idea is to get it kicked out of Scotland as a first stage. They've got a cunning plan they're very excited about, like a lot of schoolboys. No idea what, I don't ask. Better not to know.'

'Called Deep Blue?'

She looked surprised. 'There is something called Deep Blue but I don't know what. You must know more than I do.' She paused at the door. 'I probably shouldn't have mentioned any of this. You won't use it, will you?'

He shook his head. 'That sort of thing's your patch, not ours.'

'Thanks for the drink.'

They touched cheeks but he made no move to go. 'Why are you with him?' He tried to make it sound as if the question had only just occurred.

She remained still, looking at him. 'Long story.'

He nodded. 'Another time.'

Chapter Fourteen

The 1980s

Charles's memories of the Greek-liaison visit were partial but vivid, though he couldn't recall anything resembling useful liaison. He remembered the train journey to Hartlepool and how the group had fallen silent after Peterborough, sparing him the embarrassment of maintaining a stilted conversation audible to the entire first-class carriage. He stared at the wide East Midlands fields and the canal paralleling the railway, recalling that while still at school he had applied to become a lock-keeper. He had imagined a cosy cottage with a good fire and a solitary life of productive contemplation with no more than a barge a day to deflect him from poetic greatness. Oxford, the army and MI6 had knocked that out of him but the possibility of another life still lay dormant in a mental lumber room somewhere, cluttered with other forgotten fantasies.

He had three companions. The senior, Anatole,

was a youthful major from military intelligence, good-looking and with good English. The others, from civilian intelligence, were Adrienne, darkly glamorous with a flashing smile and good English, and Mikolas. Mikolas was squat and tubby, his eyes enlarged by thick-lensed spectacles. He looked as if he found the passing English scenery, trains, his coffee cup, life itself perhaps, puzzling. His English was poor. They had travelled that morning from the Castle, the training establishment on the south coast, where they had been lectured on developments in the Soviet intelligence threat and on new preventative measures. As light relief they had also been taken to the firing range to fire a variety of Russian weapons. Anatole proved to be a good shot and Adrienne an enthusiastic novice. Mikolas's glasses would not permit him to focus at the required range, nor could he see the target without them. The AK47 was taken from him after a single wandering burst. Charles suspected that Anatole had spent the night in Adrienne's room.

'We are back in London to a hotel tonight?' asked Anatole as they waited to change trains on the windswept Northallerton platform.

'No, we're staying in Hartlepool. We have a hotel there.'

Anatole smiled and exchanged glances with Adrienne.

Mikolas had two bags, whereas everyone else had

one, and there was trouble getting him off the train when they reached Hartlepool because his glasses fell under the seat. Charles had to go back and help.

'I lose my glass,' said Mikolas when they finally gained the platform.

'Yes, but it's OK now.'

'I have two bags.'

'They're both here, look.'

A Ford Transit minibus from the power station was waiting for them. The driver stacked their bags in the back except for one of Mikolas's, which he refused to release. 'I keep,' he said in wide-eyed appeal to Charles.

'You keep,' said Charles.

Anatole and Adrienne sat together in the minibus, speaking quietly in Greek. Charles felt obliged to sit with Mikolas. 'This town is historic,' he said, 'quite old.' Nineteenth-century red-brick buildings alternated with dilapidated 1960s houses and office blocks. 'Older than it looks,' he added. Then, after further thought, 'Not as old as your towns and cities, of course.'

'How old you are?'

'Not me, the town. Hartlepool. All this.' He pointed at Cameron's imposing brewery.

'I am thirty-four.'

Later, as they headed south towards the Tees estuary, Charles pointed to the steel works, where nothing much seemed to be happening. 'It used to be well-known for its fishing and its industry.'

'How old you are?'

The power station gates were open. They crossed the railway track, beyond which was a barrier, already raised. The driver barely slowed, merely waving at the man in the cubicle when he looked up from his paper. Anatole smiled and turned to Charles. 'Very good security, very quick.'

They were met by Jackie, their guide for the day. She wore a grey trouser suit and smiled whenever she spoke. In the visitor centre they were served coffee and biscuits and told they could leave their bags. The start of the briefing was delayed by Mikolas, who spent a long time in the toilet, with his bag. They were shown a short film about nuclear fission followed by another about the building of the power station.

'Now we'll start from outside and work inwards,' said Jackie. 'I'll have to ask you all to wear these badges, which are for identification only and are not indications of radiation levels. I must stress that you do not need to worry about radiation. You won't be exposed to any more than in normal life.'

Mikolas turned to Charles. 'Please explain radiation.'

Charles turned to the others. They spoke rapidly to Mikolas, who asked questions. An argument developed. All three became exasperated. 'He is worried that radiation will harm his bag,' said Anatole.

'There isn't any. We've just been told. What's in it?'

'He refuses to say.'

Mikolas appealed to Charles, wide-eyed again. 'Mr Charles, is OK?'

Charles patted him on the shoulder. 'Is OK. You can keep it.'

Mikolas hugged it to his chest with both arms as they followed Jackie, who had been holding the door open. 'Always one, isn't there?' she whispered.

They were shown the cooling chambers, the turbines, the transmission connections to the national grid and finally the control room, filled with switches and coloured lights and staff who looked like bored people trying to look like preoccupied people. There they were given another explanatory talk before returning to the briefing room for a sandwich lunch.

'When will they tell us about security?' asked Anatole.

Jackie said that the briefing request from the Foreign Office had specified an introduction to peaceful nuclear technology and had not mentioned security. Site security was another matter. There wasn't anyone who could talk on that since the whole subject was under review. Anyway, they'd all need security clearance.

Charles took a chance. 'They've got that. To a very high level.'

'They'd still need a special security briefing by someone from security.'

'Couldn't you ask someone?'

'The briefings have been stopped because of the policy review. There isn't much at the moment, anyway.'

'Much what?'

'Security. Because of the review.'

'But you must have some basic physical security we can look at, even if there's no policy.'

Jackie's smile looked increasingly strained. 'Well, there's a man on the gate. And there's the perimeter fence. It's quite high, with barbed wire on the top. I could take you to see that if you like.'

Anatole and Adrienne were whispering to each other. Mikolas was munching sandwiches, one in each hand. 'Better than nothing. Anything you can say to jazz it up a bit.'

'Or we could look at the reactor core. It's normally locked but I happen to know it's not at the moment.'

The core was in the heart of the complex, reached through several doors of which none but the last was locked. 'They're normally all locked,' said Jackie, 'but we don't bother at the moment because of the review.'

'All these doors are normally locked and guarded,' Charles told the others. 'They've been opened for us.'

They had to wait for the final door to be opened by a cross-looking, overweight woman in jeans.

'Visitors to see the rods,' said Jackie.

The woman nodded, saying nothing, and walked back to a glass-fronted box marked 'Control', where there were two other overweight women. Jackie led them on to a steel platform circling what looked like a very large metal plate punctured by holes capped by black discs. 'The rods are in there,' she said, 'inserted in the reactor to create the nuclear reaction that releases energy to drive the turbines that produce electricity.'

They all stared. Nothing moved; there appeared to be nothing happening, the chamber was still and quiet. The three women in the control box were talking and laughing but no sound came through the thick glass.

'It is safe, really?' asked Adrienne.

'Perfectly safe,' said Jackie. 'So long as the rods are in their pods. It wouldn't be safe when they're taken out. We wouldn't be allowed in then.'

Mikolas stared intently, as if he could see into the reactor core. Eventually, he turned to Charles. 'Missiles are there?'

Anatole laughed. 'He means anti-aircraft missiles.' He spoke rapidly and contemptuously to Mikolas. 'I tell him that the anti-aircraft missiles are around the perimeter, not in the reactor, and that probably we are not able to see them.'

'You're right, I'm afraid. They're not on display today.'

'If they really like radioactive things I could show them something else if it's still here,' said Jackie.

'They'd love it,' said Charles.

They were taken to a squat concrete building just inside the perimeter and surmounted by the sort of crane seen in goods yards and dockyards, a thick steel joist with a heavy pulley and supported at each end by a triangular structure, in all more than twice the width of the building and significantly higher. There was room on either side for a lorry to pull in beneath the structure. Each wall bore the large yellow radioactivity symbol and a notice on the door forbade unauthorised entry in red capitals. There was an unadorned flagpole beside it.

'Doesn't look as if it's working at the moment, so we should be allowed in,' said Jackie. 'But we'll still have to wear protective suits. Will they be all right with that?'

'I'll tell them if you can tell me what it is.'

'It's a lump of something highly radioactive which they use for blast-cleaning medical instruments and other things that have to be biologically clean. Food sometimes, so we don't get upset tummies. It's nothing to do with the power station, really. We're just a convenient place to keep it, I suppose, readily accessible, and we've got the gear to move it when it has to be replaced.'

Charles explained. 'Will it kill us?' Anatole asked with a smile.

'Not today.'

'When?' asked Mikolas.

Jackie left them outside for a few minutes then showed them into an anteroom in which white suits and masks hung on pegs, like an unusually clean rugby changing room. Jackie introduced Eric, a dapper man with neat black hair and a trim black moustache. 'Let me assure you, lady and gentlemen, that so long as you are properly attired and stand where you are told there is no danger,' he said, smiling whenever he spoke, just as Jackie did. 'Now, before we start, a brief word about what you are going to see and what it does. Forgive me if I'm teaching granny to suck eggs.'

They looked puzzled at that but Charles let it pass. Eric explained that they were going to see a lump of cobalt-60 that looked like an oversized house brick. It emitted alpha radiation, waves that passed through a substance destroying anything biological but without leaving any radioactive particle behind, so that the irradiated substance was thoroughly cleansed without itself becoming radioactive. 'If directed at you it would kill you within seconds, even at a considerable distance,' he said enthusiastically. 'That's why it could be one of the materials of choice for a dirty bomb. Something of a misnomer, really, given its cleansing properties.' He laughed and rubbed his hands. 'But you're in luck today, lady and gentlemen, because we have an array of instruments and utensils awaiting others on the conveyor belt so we can give you a brief demonstration. Now, if you would please don your suits.'

Mikolas touched Charles's arm. 'Don?'

Suited, masked, gloved and booted, they looked like astronaut snowmen. Everyone laughed behind their masks except Mikolas, who had to be persuaded by Charles to hide his bag beneath the bench. 'Otherwise it will be killed,' Charles said.

Eric led them through a steel door and down a spiral staircase on to a platform inside a circular concrete chamber, with a circular well about ten feet in diameter in the middle of the floor. Above the well was a miniature version of the hoist outside, with two taut wires running from the pulley into the water. Above that was a heavy steel trapdoor set into the ceiling. Around the perimeter of the well was a low wall with a gap on the far side. Behind the wall was a miniature version of an airport luggage conveyor belt, emerging from the platform beneath which they stood.

Eric, not yet masked, grinned at them all. 'Ready?' He turned to Adrienne. 'Would you like to press?'

'I press?'

He indicated a green button on a control panel next to him. 'You press.'

Gingerly, she did. The conveyor belt started with a click and a whirr and the pulley wires began to move. A number of silvered objects that looked like medical instruments appeared on the belt from below the platform. The colour of the well water changed from dark and opaque to something lighter, then a hint of blue, then bluer still. By the time the first of the objects reached the gap the water was almost cerulean. Just beneath the surface, suspended by wires, was a rectangular lump about a foot long and so blue it seemed the source of all blueness. The only sound was the faint slither of the belt.

Eric turned to Charles, his voice now muffled by his mask. 'Now you can say you've seen the most radioactive source in Britain. Deep Blue, it's called. Boil your liver, it would. In seconds.'

'What did you call it?'

Chapter Fifteen

The Present

Charles met Sue in the cafeteria in the crypt of St John's, Smith Square, convenient for her office in Thames House. 'Never seem to get out for lunch these days,' she said, as they queued at the self-service counter. 'Not like it used to be years ago when we first met and everyone went out to lunch. Now we have sandwiches at our desks. Makes us a dull lot, not enough play. Surprised the great C has time for lunches.'

'I do almost nothing but. Official visitors and whatever. Makes a change to get out and see someone I actually want to see.'

'Don't tell me it's for my beautiful blue eyes. You must want something else now. No thanks.'

She was refusing the offer of wine. 'Yes, we will,' said Charles. 'A bottle of Sauvignon.'

She looked askance. 'Knocks me out in the afternoons. You'll have to drink most of it.'

'I probably shall.'

They took their trays to a table in an alcove that once held coffins. 'So, what is it?' she asked. 'D'you want more vetting files sent over? Did you get the ones I sent?'

'I did, thanks. Haven't read them all properly yet, just skimmed. I was hoping they'd have more in them about James Micklethwaite than they do. Would the rest be on his personal file? He must have had one.'

'He did indeed: Trotsky Jim. Still a political groupie now, isn't he? But I couldn't legitimately call for it even if it still exists, which it probably doesn't, unless we were properly vetting him or his lady friend. And you're not proposing that, are you? Supposedly, you just wanted basic tracing details. I sent you more than I should, anyway.'

'But she must have been vetted, mustn't she? Given what she now has access to.'

'As a SPAD she gets routine clearance up to Secret. The Home Office wouldn't have bothered with any more. Now she's with us she ought to be fully vetted and I put it up to the DDG but still haven't got an answer. You know what Simon's like; they're all like that now. Terrified of being accused of anything ideo-logical. Combating Cold War subversion is now seen as spying on loyal patriotic trade unionists, which it never was, KGB spies like Jack Jones et al notwithstanding. What more d'you want to know about Trotsky Jim, anyway? Not thinking of resuming relations with his sister, I hope?' She smiled.

'I want to test your memory of our trip to the North East. See if it accords with mine.'

'Oh, God, that was a century ago. Why?'

'Because I think it holds the key to something going on now.'

'Sounds like a two-glass subject.' She poured them both more wine. 'Go on, take me back there.'

The 1980s

Charles recalled that once he had settled the group into their Hartlepool hotel, he had rung the SIS switchboard in search of Hookey, who couldn't be contacted, then the MI5 duty officer in search of Sue, who also couldn't be found. He left messages for both. The next problem was what to do with his charges while he called on James, notionally to retrieve his book. Janet had arranged with James that he would call at about seven. His charges, meanwhile, had indicated that they wanted a typically English dinner. Silently despairing, Charles flicked through the tourist guide in his room and called the concierge, who recommended a new place down by the dock called Roast Beef&Frills. He didn't much like the sound of it when he rang but was assured of typically English fare, as interpreted by the tourist industry. He booked a table for nine o'clock, allowing time for his call and for Anatole and Adrienne to enjoy the pre-prandial session they so obviously desired. Neither answered their phones, so he was reduced to knocking first on Anatole's door, then on Adrienne's. Anatole answered at the third knock, a bath towel around his hips. Charles explained, unable to suppress a smile. Anatole smilingly thanked him and said that they were both too tired to go out and would put up with room service 'in our rooms'.

Charles returned to find Mikolas at his door, clutching his bag. 'I am ready.'

'Good, good. The others won't be joining us. They're busy.'

'They are tired. We go to typical English pub?'

'Something like that.'

'We go now, please?'

'Are you sure you don't want to rest first?'

'I am ready.'

'I'll have to leave you there because I have to see someone before dinner. Are you sure you wouldn't rather wait here?'

'I am ready.'

The streets of Hartlepool were almost deserted and there was a pervasive smell of chips. The tourist map was grossly oversimplified. 'It is longer? How much?' asked Mikolas after about twenty minutes.

'Not long now.'

'I have been here before. Already I have seen this church.'

He was right but Charles didn't want to admit it. 'Churches are very similar in Hartlepool.' He had seen only one other, which was quite different.

'Always I am with my bag.'

'I've noticed. What's in it?'

'My book. I am writing book about the psychology of the world, of all people.'

'That sounds very interesting.'

'There are no people in my book because our psychology, we all share, we are all one.'

'Of course.'

'You would like to read my book?'

'Very much. Here we are, look. Over the road.'

It was an incongruous black and white mock-Tudor building not far from the fish dock. The central portion was red brick, all that remained of the former pub which had turned itself into a club and now charged for entry. Inside were tables with red lamps and shades, with a wide bar in the gloom beyond.

'You can sit here in the bar until I get back,' said Charles. 'Then we'll go into the restaurant and eat. I'll sit with you while we order drinks.' He was anticipated by a waiter with an ice-bucket and champagne. 'I don't think—'

'Champagne good,' said Mikolas, smiling for the first time.

Two girls in high heels, black stockings and suspenders, knickers and bras appeared behind the waiter.

'Thank you,' said Charles, 'but I don't think—'

Mikolas's laugh was startling, like the bark of muntjac in Charles's native Chiltern beech woods. The waiter poured champagne and the girls sat. 'I'm Jane,' one said to Mikolas. 'What's your name, love?'

'I'm Jennifer,' the other said to Charles. She was older than her companion, with wrinkles around her mouth and eyes and stretch-marks on her breasts. 'What company are you with, love?'

'My own, it's my company.'

She paused with her glass at her lips. 'Not paying yourself, are you?'

This was a woman he could do business with. 'Tell me the score.'

She lowered her voice. 'You're drinking a hundred quid from this bottle. Then there's the table charge, another hundred. Then there's us two and we don't come cheap. Then there's dinner. Then if you want extras, which your friend looks as if he might . . .'

Jane was provocatively refilling Mikolas's glass, making the most of her cleavage.

Charles slipped a folded twenty-pound note across to Jennifer. 'Thanks for that. I'd better get him out of here.'

She slid the note into her knickers. 'Best we go first, otherwise the bouncers won't let you out. You'll still have to pay for the bottle and table.'

'My problem is I've got to leave him here while I go to another meeting for an hour and a half. Anywhere nearby you can suggest? Somewhere not too expensive but where he'd be happy to wait?'

She leaned forward, as if in intimate conversation.

'The Fishermens Bar here, other end of the building. It's just a bar, no food but the booze is cheaper and one of us can pop through now and again to keep an eye on him, make him feel a bit wanted.'

'Perfect.' He slipped her another note.

The Fishermens Bar was adorned with nineteenth century sea-scapes, ropes and netting. Charles put Mikolas in a corner with a bottle of house wine. 'I shall be about an hour and a half. You can write your novel.'

'You go with Jane?'

'No, nothing like that. I'm going to a meeting.'

'With Jennifer?'

James's flat was a short minicab ride away, inland from the brewery and on the ground floor of a small 1960s block. He and Charles had last met over Sunday lunch at his and Janet's parents' house in Surrey. They had been as civil with each other as it was possible to be without any meeting of minds. This time, each appeared exactly as the other would caricature him. James answered the door wearing jeans deliberately holed in the knees and a floppy roll-necked jumper. His hair was in a ponytail and he had not shaved. Charles was wearing tweed jacket, corduroys and tie. He couldn't help smiling at their mutual self-caricatures. There was immediate and forced good cheer on both sides.

James led him into a sitting room dominated by a nuclear-disarmament poster on the wall and smelling strongly of curry and cigarettes. Charles's copy of *Beware of Pity* was on a drink-ringed coffee table by the ashtray. 'I've been meaning to give it to Janet for ages,' James said. 'I remember it whenever I see her but not before.'

'There was never any hurry. I only thought of it when I knew I had to be in this area. You're working up here now, Janet tells me?' He regretted the 'up' since to anyone looking for cause for resentment it could imply that the centre of gravity, the natural place to be, was in the South.

James seemed not to notice. 'Supply teaching in a local comp. Tea, coffee?'

This was better than Charles had anticipated. 'What brings you here, anyway?' James called from the kitchen.

'Bear-leading a foreign delegation. Showing them there's more to Britain than Buckingham Palace.' Among the papers on the table was a flier about the Greenham Common protest camp.

'What, walking them round ruined abbeys and all that?'

'That sort of thing.'

'Janet said you were visiting some radar installation.'

'That too.'

They sat in a couple of comfortable well-worn armchairs. James rolled a cigarette, grinning. 'So, how's the Establishment?'

'Still there.'

'You must be a pillar of it now, in the Foreign Office and all that?'

'Roof-tile, more like.'

'Ever thought of doing anything else?'

'Not seriously, no. I must be unimaginative or unambitious. Public service of some sort always seemed the natural thing. I guess for you too, given what you're doing?'

'Bit of difference between teaching children, trying to improve deprived lives, and what you do, propping up the system.'

Charles grinned back. 'You think there really is a system?'

They knocked the subject back and forth amicably enough at first, like tennis players warming up. James insisted on a worldwide capitalist conspiracy against the have-nots, Charles on the social good of individual freedoms as opposed to the coercion of community. They were interrupted by the phone, which was on the window ledge. James answered it facing out of the window, his back to Charles. The pause between his first 'hello' and his second suggested the caller was putting coins in. The conversation was brief, with James's part confined to a 'no', a 'yes' and – twice – 'OK'. He remained facing the window, giving Charles the chance to glance at other papers on the coffee table. One was a price-list from a local commercial-vehicle-hire company, with the handwritten addition of a price for an 'Iveco 7.5-tonne tail-lift with forklift'. He was still trying to make it out when James put down the phone, without saying goodbye.

James sat again. 'So what are you going to do after the revolution?'

'Join the counter-revolution.'

'If you're not put up against a wall and shot first, like most of this government will be. Should be.' He began rolling another cigarette. 'You know you're taking a risk with your security clearance, coming here? Special Branch will know. They spy on me.'

'Do they?'

'Flat was broken into last month. Must have been them. Clumsy job, nothing was taken. They must have been looking for something.'

'You really think that?' The conversation was reverting to a familiar path. As on previous occasions, Charles was inclined at first to assume that James was being facetious, as perhaps he was, but after a while it became apparent that he meant his assertions to be taken seriously. Charles had once told him that he was being preposterous when James claimed he was on an MI5 hit list and likely to be assassinated, but it had made no difference. James's combination of intelligence and conspiratorial credulity was something Charles had often discussed with Janet who, though critical of her brother, felt obliged to defend him against mockery. He had upset her by arguing that James's ideological rigidity warped his judgement in all areas of life, making it impossible to take him seriously about anything.

'I do really think it, yes, I do,' James said.

His earnestness was such that Charles had to stop himself smiling. 'What could you have here that Special Branch couldn't get anywhere else and wanted so badly that they broke in to get it?'

This time James smiled through a cloud of smoke. 'You don't think I'm going to tell you, do you?'

Charles changed tack, asking James about his social life, whether he had friends locally or relied on visitors from London, then left before the conversation became too strained. Unable to find a cab, he eventually got a bus that took him not far from the Roast Beef&Frills. He rang the SIS switchboard from the callbox in the foyer, again without getting hold of Hookey or Sue.

Mikolas was sitting where he'd left him, hugging his bag and seemingly comatose, empty bottle and two glasses on the table before him. When his enlarged eyes blinked open, Charles said, 'Thank you for waiting. We can eat now. I hope you weren't too bored.'

'Jane comes.'

'She came to see you? That was nice of her. Now we can have dinner.'

'She comes again if I am here. We go to her house.'

'I don't think so. She's busy now.'

'I wait.'

'It's too late, they're about to close. Jane has to go home to her husband and children. And her parents and his parents. We can have dinner at our hotel. You can tell me about your novel.'

It took a while to move him. Charles's assertion of imminent closure was not helped by the arrival of taxi-loads of customers, but luckily Mikolas was by then engrossed in his description of his novel. During dinner he explained how dispensing with characters enabled him to evoke the full range and depth of human psychology and directly access the universal spirit of mankind. Charles almost embraced the concierge, who interrupted: 'Telephone call for Mr Thoroughgood.'

'Where the hell have you been?'

It could only be Hookey. 'In Hartlepool with that Greek liaison I was telling you about. I've been trying to ring—'

'Thought you were at the Castle. No one there had a clue where you were. I had to get hold of old Harold. Useless, complete waste of space, always was. Your new controller was no better. Irritated by the mere mention of you, which was some satisfaction. In the end I tracked down your oppo, what's-his-name ...'

'Mike.'

'Another waste of space. But at least he knew.'

'He was supposed to be doing it. I was lumbered with it because—'

'Point is, your friend's arriving in town first thing tomorrow. Not for his op yet, that's later. He's in Paris now. Can't send you there to meet him again after the debacle last time so I used an industry contact to invite him here to talk to BAE about picking up any crumbs from the table of his deal with the French. My contact's sticking his neck out for us by getting you into the talks as Foreign Office rep. Foreign Office knows nothing about it, of course. Sort that out afterwards. It'll be up to you to engineer a minute alone with him to see if there's any more light he can shed on this Deep Blue thing. Maybe no-go, but worth a try so long as you don't do anything damn foolish and compromise him. My contact knows nothing of all this, of course. Thinks you're just there to find out about Soviet aerospace requirements.'

Charles checked that the concierge was involved with another customer, then said quietly, 'I know what Deep Blue is. I've seen it. At least, I've seen something called it.'

Hookey listened. 'Have you told your Gower Street friends?'

'Not yet, I've been trying to.'

'Make sure they know asap. They may have some idea why the other side want it. Must have plenty of cobalt-60 of their own, more than we have. No idea why they want ours, what they could do with it?'

'No, but I did wonder if—'

'You must still meet your friend tomorrow. He may enlighten us. Get the first train down. Meeting's at ten in my contact's office, Euston Road. Go to Gower Street first.'

'But I'm supposed to be with the liaison group.'

'They can find their own way to the station without you. Tell them you've been summoned by the Prime Minister or the Queen or any damn thing. Just make sure you're there.' He hung up.

Charles returned to the table. 'I wish to sleep, please,' said Mikolas.

'Good. I mean, so do I, it's good to sleep.' He explained that he had been summoned to London early in the morning and would meet them at their London hotel later that day.

'On the train I write my novel.'

'Good, splendid.'

The remains of two dinners on trays were outside Adrienne's room. Charles's first knock was answered by a firm, 'No, thank you.'

'Anatole, it's me, Charles.'

Anatole wore his towel again. Charles explained. 'OK,' said Anatole, and closed the door.

Charles dreamed that night that he was in a barber's shop being shaved by James, with Sue in the background dressed like the hostesses of the Roast Beef&Frills but in underclothes of pulsating blue. He was reading Mikolas's novel.

Chapter Sixteen

The 1980s

The meeting was on one of the upper floors of the Euston tower block, above the two occupied by A4, MI5's surveillance section. It was a short walk from Gower Street where Charles had been to brief Sue.

'You're going to tell me you've identified Deep Blue,' she said.

'Well ...'

'And it's a lump of cobalt-60 used to irradiate things with alpha radiation.' She laughed. 'You look like a dog that's lost its bone. Don't worry, I didn't work it out for myself. Your Hookey told Director K who told me. And now you're off to some meeting I'm not allowed to know about to find out what the Russians want to do with it.'

'Not find out, more likely.'

'Meanwhile, the Turnips are on the move again. Last night, Mr Turnip made another call to your friend James.'

'I think I was with him when he took it.'

'Good. Tell me all in a minute.'

'I've only got a minute.'

'This time we know what was said. We've got a warrant on James's number. The Turnips are getting a train to Hartlepool tonight to meet James in connection with something they're planning tomorrow. We're asking the local Special Branch to put them under surveillance and Director K wants me to go up there to brief them. Hookey says you're to go as well. To keep an eye on me, I s'pose.'

'But I've only just got back from Hartlepool and I've still got these liaison visitors I'm supposed to—'

'Well, aren't you just a lucky boy, so much in demand. Someone else wants you, too – got a note here somewhere – yes, C/Europe, Angus something, wants to speak to you urgently. Sounded annoyed that you were coming here first. Here's his number.'

Angus would have to wait. The meeting was chaired by Hookey's contact, CEO of a specialist aeronautical electronics company. It comprised his marketing manager, a man introduced as 'our top boffin' and Federov plus five other Russians. Like Americans, Russians were always heavily over-represented in international fora. Charles, who had not had time to go home and change, was the only one not wearing a suit. He had been introduced as 'Foreign Office with a brief from the Board of Trade' and had solemnly shaken hands with each of the unsmiling Russians. Federov had greeted him with dismissive hauteur, as if doing his host a favour by acknowledging a junior official. During a pause in the CEO's account of what his company could do for aerospace, coffee and biscuits were replenished and the CEO took Federov to the window, pointing out features of London.

'We have such things also in Moscow,' said Federov. He asked for the toilet. The CEO bade the marketing manager escort him.

Charles slipped out of the other door and followed them to the loo, where Federov was in one of the cubicles. Charles joined the marketing manager at the urinal. When they had finished they returned to the corridor to await Federov.

'I'll see him back if you like,' said Charles. The manager left, Charles waited to hear the toilet flush, then went back in. Federov was washing his hands. The other cubicles were empty.

'How is your health?'

'I am waiting to hear when is the operation. I have to finish my pills first, which will be after next week.'

'Last time, you mentioned something called Deep Blue. I think I now know what it is. Do you know why the KGB wants it and what they intend to do with it?'

Federov's eyes met his in the mirror. 'Is this why there is this meeting – for you to meet me?'

'Partly why. There is a serious business purpose.'

'You know it is very dangerous for me.'

'We are worried about Deep Blue.'

He turned to face Charles as he dried his hands, clearly angry. 'I am not your slave. I am not your creature. I help you because you help me. Also because my government is corrupt. The government is the state, the state is Russia, Russia is corrupt. But I am not your creature.'

'We know that, we never expected you to be. We want a relationship of equals. You advise us when you feel you can, we help you when you need it.' He did not relish going back to Hookey and confessing that he had lost the case.

'And if one day I want to bring my family here, to live here, you will still help? You have promised.'

'We have and we shall.'

Federov continued to stare into Charles's eyes, before resuming more calmly. 'This thing, Deep Blue, I don't know what it is, what they want to do with it. I am not KGB, you know that.'

'But who told you about it? When? Who else was there? What were the exact words? What was the context?'

Federov waited for footsteps in the corridor to fade. 'It was at the Central Committee last month, not in the meeting but afterwards at lunch. I was with Lipinski. You know him? He is KGB, First Chief Directorate, responsible for foreign intelligence, like your MI6. His desk officer for Britain and Scandinavia department brings him a message, which he reads, and afterwards he smiles, and says, "We are making trouble for England, for the English government. We will kidnap their Deep Blue and give them headache, big headache." I ask what is Deep Blue, and he laughs and says, "Don't worry, you will read about it. It will be news, big news. Bad news for England." That is all I know.'

Charles nodded. They shook hands again. 'Thank you, Igor. You must get back to the meeting. We won't go together. I'll come later.'

Federov was in no hurry. 'Now I have something I must ask you. The camp where I was prisoner, the camp where I knew Josef. I have been back. It is empty now, closed, there are only the old guards there. They are the real prisoners now. One day I will write book about the camp but first I would like photographs of it. Does MI6 have some? Can you get them for me, please?'

Charles doubted it but thought there might be some in an archive somewhere, Amnesty International, perhaps, or the Americans. The Americans had photographed pretty well everything. 'I'll look for it. We have the camp number, Josef told us. You will ring me when you come out for your operation?'

'I will ring. But please, please.' He half smiled. 'No more invented invitations, Charles.'

Later, back in Century House, Charles climbed the stairs to his office to write up the meeting for Hookey, hoping by ignoring the lifts to avoid Angus

Copplestone, whose office was near them. He would leave a message for Angus, anticipating that, like most people, he would lunch out or in the twentieth-floor restaurant. Angus had lost no opportunity to lunch out in Paris, usually with visitors or colleagues who might be useful to him. Charles hoped to be on his way back to Hartlepool by the time Angus tried to contact him.

But Angus appeared in his doorway. 'Charles, nice to see you at last. Have you got a moment?' He didn't wait for a response.

Charles followed him. Angus asked him to shut the connecting door to his secretary's office but did not invite him to sit. His pale face was perhaps a little paler than usual. It struck Charles that Angus might relish the encounter no more than he did. He decided to take the initiative by being conciliatory. 'I'm sorry to have been so elusive. I was in Hartlepool with the Greek liaison visitors and then was called back in connection with the Sovbloc operation I've been helping with. I should have made sure more people knew where I was.'

'Presumably the same operation that led to your fracas in Paris? And meanwhile, have you any idea where the liaison visitors you're supposedly looking after actually are?'

'They should be on the train on their way back from Hartlepool.'

'So you simply left them there, you abandoned them? On C/Sovbloc's bidding?' His tone was the familiar resentful one of those not involved in Sovbloc operations. 'Makes a change from the demands of your personal life, I suppose. You're aware, of course, that your visitors were due at the Greek Embassy for lunch today?'

Charles remembered as Angus said it. He had failed to remind himself of the final day's programme. 'I was but I'd forgotten. I apologise. Are they not there?'

'They are not. Nor have they checked in to their London hotel. The Greek Ambassador has been on to the Foreign Office and the military attaché on to me. My secretary rang your Hartlepool hotel only to find that two of them are still in bed and the other checked out hours ago but no one knows where to. It's a complete mess and a serious embarrassment and it's your fault, Thoroughgood.'

The use of surname in a service in which all but the Chief were called by their first names, and in which people were asked rather than ordered to act, was a mark of grave displeasure. 'Again, I apologise. I hadn't planned to return without them, as you know, They knew which train they were booked on and I told them I would catch up with them today. But I failed to check the programme.'

'Nor did you tell anyone.'

'Both Harold and Mike were away.' He didn't know whether Harold was actually away but his evasions were sufficiently habitual to amount to the same thing. 'I should have thought to ring you. I'm sorry.' He paused. 'As a matter of fact, I have to return to

Hartlepool tonight, on the same operation. I'll find them if they haven't turned up by then.'

'They're probably on their way back now. Someone else will have to see them off tomorrow. I may have to do it myself. This won't be forgotten, Thoroughgood.'

'I accept responsibility. I'm sorry.' Not for the first time, he was aware that he found apologising suspiciously easy, as if perhaps he didn't care enough. Where Angus was concerned, he didn't.

'I shall write an addendum to your annual confidential report. I shall also request you be posted away from this section, as you were from Paris. My only regret is that you're not still on probation.'

Probation lasted three years, with permanent status conferred only at the end. Charles nodded. He wasn't surprised. 'Is there anything else?'

He had meant that, if Angus had any further criticisms, they may as well be voiced now, but it was clear from Angus's whitening face and knuckles that he interpreted it as insolence. For a few seconds he said nothing, then, in little more than a whisper, he said, 'Get out of my office.'

Chapter Seventeen

The Present

Simon Mall had a large office in Thames House with a river view, accessed via the private secretaries' room, as was the DG's office on the other side. Charles had asked his own private secretary, Elaine, to arrange his call on Simon for a time when Melanie Stokes was not in the building.

'Took some doing,' she said. 'I had to pretend you wanted to see her too, make an appointment and then try to move it, which meant they had to say when she wasn't around. Then I had to make another appointment with her and then cancel that, saying you'd pop in for a quick chat with Simon instead. They're pretty fed up with me up there.'

'You'll be rewarded in heaven.'

'I'd rather have lunch.'

'Come up with me. You must have friends in the building you could push off with while I'm with Simon.'

Meeting Simon always reminded Charles of the P.G. Wodehouse character who looked as if once in his life he had missed a train, and the thought had preyed upon him ever since. Since Michael Dunton's heart attack and the imposition of Melanie Stokes his complexion had become as grey as his suit and his thin hair. 'How are things with Melanie?' asked Charles, cheerfully.

Simon glanced warily at the closed door. 'She's moved into Michael's office. It was always obvious that she thought of herself as DG but now other people are beginning to as well. It's all I can do to keep everything from going to her.'

'Well, I've got a story to tell which mustn't on any account go to her.' Simon's frown deepened. 'Don't worry, it's nothing that the Service has done or not done. The reason's more to do with her.' He had discussed the whole thing over dinner with Sarah the night before, telling her everything. It was more to clear his own mind than for anything she could contribute, since she had little knowledge of the people involved and none at all of those past events which he was convinced held the clue to what was happening now. Her questioning acted as a mental detergent and he emerged with his next step clarified: he should tell all to MI5 in order to alert them and formally request their help, despite the risk that it might get back to Melanie. That way, if they did help and kept it from her, all well and good; they had all the tools for the job, the statutory right to do it and it was much more their patch than his. If they did not and he acted unofficially, as he was prepared to do, he could at least argue to any subsequent inquiry that he had tried to follow proper procedures and been rebuffed.

'The story starts with an old Russian case,' he told Simon, 'that became a joint case between both our services. Inconclusive and long dead now.' He recounted everything to do with the Melburys, Josef and Federov. As he was finishing Simon had to take a call from the Metropolitan Police Commissioner complaining about MI5's refusal to do something.

Simon repeated the refusal and put down the phone with a sigh. 'Always wanting us to do more than we can. If we agreed to investigate every instance of rhetorical Islamist extremism we'd have no time to look at terrorists actually planning attacks. We have to go for the crocodiles nearest the boat. If I've said that once I've said it a hundred times. Go on with your story, please. So nice to hear something historic. Quite restful, really.' He smiled.

'Well, now I'm afraid I have to bring you back to the present. I think some – one, anyway – of those involved before are planning the same thing again.'

'But you never ascertained exactly what it was they were planning?'

'True, but going back through the files I think I've worked out what it was or might have been. More or less, anyway. The difficulty, the political difficulty, is that the principal, the person most involved now as he was years ago, is Melanie's partner, the journalist and Triple A activist James Micklethwaite. And that he seems to be doing it with someone on the far-out fringes of Triple A. Someone the Foreign Secretary's SPAD says was kicked out of the SNP for wanting separation with violence.'

Simon visibly stiffened at the mention of the SNP. As Charles continued, his tired face settled into a mask of judicious and contented non-commitment. When Charles finished he put his hands together, fingertip to fingertip as if in prayer, and said, 'If you are right about what they intend – a big "If" – and if they manage it this time – which is by no means certain, given their performance last time – what do you suppose they want to do with it? Even in their wildest moments, Triple A and SNP renegades are not in the market for mass casualties, unlike the crocodiles we deal with every day.'

'I'm not sure what they intend.' In fact, Charles was pretty sure he knew, but if he told Simon and Simon still did not agree to take it on, his own freedom of action would be compromised. 'That's what we need to find out.'

Simon shook his head. Reasons for inaction came easily to him. 'I see your argument, Charles, and you're right to be concerned, but essentially what you have is a theory, not evidence, and a theory about a possible aspiration, not a plot, not attack planning.

And with the final bit – the aim, what they want to
achieve – missing. Also, as you well know, we put
all that political subversion stuff behind us long ago.
We simply don't do it now and if it amounts to law-
breaking it's for the police. Nor do we go anywhere
near British political parties, however wild the outer
fringes. So I'm afraid it's a no-no.' He clasped his
hands and smiled, as if in celebration of an achieve-
ment. 'Sorry, Charles.'

It was what Charles had expected and he knew that
argument would be futile. They discussed the terrorist
threat for a while, with Simon saying that the UK was
due an attack. Charles enquired after Michael Dunton,
the DG; the heart bypass had been a success, he was
expected home shortly, convalescence would be at least
six months, he was talking of returning to work but it
was not known whether he would.

Elaine was waiting for him downstairs. 'Good
meeting?'

'Objective achieved. Good lunch?'

'Lovely lunch. An old friend who joined with me
then transferred here and now runs one of their
A4 – surveillance – sections. Sounds fun. Odd hours,
though.'

They were back in Croydon in time for the weekly
main board meeting, at which Elaine took the minutes.
'Message from Sarah,' she said as they were about to
go in. 'She says please call. It's about what you were
discussing last night.'

'I'll catch you up.'

Sarah was busy and brief. 'Deep Blue, your Deep Blue. I think I know where it's kept now, the one in current use, anyway. I was going through some of our industrial injuries claims and came across a reference to it. It's on an industrial estate outside Newcastle. I'll bring the address home, shall I?'

After the meeting he rang Sue in MI5, but it was one of her non-working days. He persisted and was put through to her at home. 'D'you know anyone at Northumberland SB? If not, could you tell me the best way to contact them. Informally.'

She chuckled. 'Don't give up, do you? As a matter of fact, I do. So do you. H/SB is Bob Shea, whom we dealt with all those years ago, remember? He was new to it, then. Mind you, we all were.'

The 1980s

He remembered Bob clearly, a young SB officer from Durham. The file recorded that staff shortages meant that Cleveland Police SB were temporarily housed at that time with Northumbria Police, and they had to travel to Newcastle to see him. Police HQ was outside the city, a collection of large detached older houses built around a green. They had once comprised a children's home and SB were allocated two attic bedrooms.

'Jim's on leave and Rob's on a course,' said the fresh-faced Bob. 'So you'll have to make do with the new boy, I'm afraid. Tea, coffee?'

Sue had described their business by telegram before they left London for Newcastle. 'James Micklethwaite is still at home in Hartlepool as far as we know. At least, he was when we left. Trouble is, he's not on live monitoring so we have to wait for his line to be transcribed. And we've no idea where the Melburys are. They rang to get the price and times of returns to Hartlepool but didn't book. Made no hotel booking, either. So we've assumed they're here anyway and that they're meeting James. Most unlikely that they're staying with him given the efforts they've made to keep their links clandestine.'

Bob made a note on his pad. 'We can easily check hotels. Are they likely to use that name?'

'No indication so far of their using other identities. Is it possible to put anyone on to James Micklethwaite?'

'Well, there's only me and I'm afraid he might remember me. I arrested him a couple of years ago before I joined the Branch. He was on a peace demo outside the Vickers works here in Newcastle. Chucked a brick at a police horse, let off with a caution. But we had a bit of an argy-bargy in the van, so he'd probably remember me. Cocky bugger.'

They agreed that Charles and Sue would try to find out whether he was at home. Sue checked with her office that there had been no further activity on his line. 'We'd better find a hotel for ourselves,' said Charles.

'Not till we know where the Melburys are staying, if anywhere. Don't want them in the room next door. They saw me at your place, remember.'

'You need some wheels,' said Bob. 'I could run you down there to have a quick look at his place but you couldn't hang around without a car. It's quite a distance anyway. I'll take you now to a car-hire place we use and we can drive down in convoy.'

Later, they waited in a hired blue Triumph Acclaim, out of sight of James's ground-floor windows but within sight of the entrance to his block of Hartlepool flats. Their cruise past had not revealed whether he was in and they had decided against risking a wrong-number call to check.

'Who's this other bloke you asked Bob to check hotels for?' asked Sue. 'The foreign one. How many operations are you doing today?'

'A missing Greek,' Charles explained.

'No wonder your boss was angry. There's Bob.'

The arrangement was that if Bob had anything to report he'd cruise past in the opposite direction in his unmarked police Sierra and they'd follow him to the Co-op car park a couple of miles away.

'The Melburys are booked into the hotel where you stayed with your foreign visitors,' said Bob. 'Three nights, usual amount of luggage. Quite chatty at reception, he was, anyway. Said they were hiring a car and doing a bit of walking on the moors. Your other friend, the Greek one, is still booked in too though they haven't seen much of him. Not worried because they reckon the Foreign Office is paying. What d'you reckon he's up to?'

'Probably looking for a lady-friend in the Roast Beef&Frills.'

'Well, if he can't find one there he's in a bad way. Or out of money. It may be that's where the Melburys have gone to eat. They left on foot half an hour ago, saying they were going to eat somewhere local. I can check that out for you if you like. See if your Romeo's there too.'

They cruised past James's flat before parking again. It was dark by now and there was one light on in the flat, which meant nothing.

'He doesn't have a car, does he?' Sue asked.

'A brown Allegro, he mentioned it, I remember now. Just got it, second-hand. But I never saw it and don't know the number.'

She stared at him. 'Why didn't you say so, you chump? There was one earlier, parked with those other cars on his side of the road. V-registered, I think, so not new. We could have asked Bob to check the Roast Beef&Frills car park.'

He held up his hands. 'Might as well go and check it ourselves. Mea culpa.'

'What's that supposed to mean?'

They spotted the brown Allegro near the entrance to the car park and parked as far away from it as possible. They couldn't see Bob's car. 'Hope he hasn't gone back to look for us,' said Sue.

'He can't have been here that long and may have parked elsewhere. I'll take a chance and poke my head inside.'

'Don't forget your wig and moustache. You lot always carry them, don't you?'

The foyer was disappointingly empty so he attached himself to a group of four studying the menu outside the restaurant on the right. The bar was on the left, impossible to see in without entering. When the group moved on to the restaurant he tagged along behind them until he had a view of the tables. Neither the Melburys nor James were there. He took another chance and crossed reception to the bar entrance, where he paused. Bob was at the bar with his back to Charles, talking to the barman. There was no point risking going farther, since Bob would know whether they were there, so he walked briskly out, crossing the car park to the street and reflecting, not for the first time, how difficult it was to do anything even mildly clandestine without feeling and looking as if you were doing something worse, such as reconnoitring on behalf of an IRA bombing team.

Bob's Sierra was parked across the road near a bus-stop. Charles waited as if for a bus until Bob returned, then approached him. Bob started. 'Christ, didn't see you there. Jump in. Sorry about the baby clutter.' He threw a tiny blue glove and a plastic rattle on to the back seat. 'They're in the bar, the Melburys and our lad Jim. It was just the Melburys at first, there when I got there; I reckoned it must be them because the barman – old friend, as it were – thought they were

DEEP BLUE

American. I was going to sit near them but was pre-empted by another couple, luckily because two minutes later in comes our lad to join them. Fortunately, I was still at the bar and he didn't see me, fairly sure he didn't, anyway. He sits down with them without getting a drink, then after about a minute they all get up and go into the restaurant. The barman told me they'd booked a table for three and he could fix us a window table close by if we want. But we're all a bit too well known, aren't we?'

Charles thought. 'If we could find my missing Greek, we could use him.'

'Would he be any good?'

'Not by himself. We'd need to put Sue with him if she's up for it.'

They walked back to the Acclaim. Charles explained to Sue. 'But how could I?' she said. 'They've met me. On the stairs in your flat.'

Charles sensed Bob registering that. 'Only that once and fleetingly. People often don't recognise people out of context. And you've had your hair cut since then.'

'Nice of you to notice.'

'And you could put it up, couldn't you? Do something with it, anyway.'

She looked doubtful. 'What's he like, your Greek friend?'

'Just your sort.'

*

205

He found Mikolas, as expected, in the club part of the establishment. He was at a table with a woman, not one Charles recognised from the other night but similarly attired. His bag was on the bench next to him and he had not shaved. His expression when he saw Charles was mingled consternation and appeasement.

Charles smiled reassuringly. 'Mikolas, I'd like you to meet a friend of mine who wants to have dinner with you.'

'No, I have—'

'This gentleman has booked his dinner with me,' said the woman. 'He's a regular, he comes here every night.'

Charles slipped a twenty-pound note beneath her champagne glass. 'He's booked next door as well. Come on, Mikolas.'

Mikolas shook his head. 'No, I stay here, I—'

'There's another lady waiting for you. She's a publisher. She wants to hear about your book.'

Ten minutes later, Mikolas and Sue were at the window table near the Melburys and James. Table separation, which professional habit had made for Charles the determining criterion in restaurant choice, was not good; which meant it was good for listeners. Both tables could be seen from the car park.

Sue had acquiesced without enthusiasm. 'But there's no guarantee they're going to discuss their dastardly plans, whatever they are, over dinner, is there? And the fact that they're meeting in public now is either bad tradecraft or it suggests they're not trying to hide anything. Not here, anyway. And if I've got to chat up your Greek friend at the same time – what's his English like? And what does he think I am, a tart or a publisher?'

'Both, probably.'

'Well, if he thinks there's going to be any après-ski he's got another think coming.' She was getting out of the car as she spoke. 'I'll get you back for this, Charles Thoroughgood. You wait.'

'Hang on, we need to agree where we're to meet afterwards. You'd better drop him back at his hotel—'

'I'm not staying there.'

'. . . and I'll find somewhere for us to stay.'

'I know a place,' said Bob. 'I know the manager.'

'And now it's raining and I haven't got an umbrella,' said Sue.

The hotel was a faded low-rise 1960s block overlooking the docks and a building site. 'No point in you hanging around as well unless you've got no home to go to,' Charles told Bob.

Bob raised his eyebrows. 'Say that again. I'm already in trouble for working late. She thinks I do it for fun, as if I'm having a bit of hookey, like. I daren't tell her one of you's a woman, never hear the last of it. Give you a call first thing.'

Charles checked the rooms Bob had arranged for them then sat in reception flicking through the day's papers. His overnight bag and book were in the boot of the hire car. The dining room had plastic tables and chairs, loud music and two diners, so when the rain left off he decided to walk into town to eat. The only people in the wet streets seemed to be drinkers hurrying from one pub to the next. He lingered outside several, which were either too busy or deserted and unappetising, until the return of the rain drove him into a Chinese restaurant. He emerged bloated and unsatisfied an hour later. The rain fell steadily as he trudged back to the hotel, where he read the adverts in the local paper until roused by Sue.

'Sorry to wake you.'

'I wasn't asleep.'

'You were, you were nodding.' She looked pleased with herself and took the armchair next to his, unpinning her hair and shaking her head. 'This place looks all right. We've got rooms? Gin and tonic, please. Reckon I deserve it.'

She had reason to be pleased with herself. 'It was awful at first, couldn't hear a thing from the Turnips or Mikolas because there was a noisy lot at another table and you know how quietly he speaks. The Turnips and James weren't exactly shouting, either. Anyway, the other party left as the waiter came for our orders, which meant long pauses because Mikolas took so long to decide, bless him. I heard Mr Turnip say, "When do you pick it up?" And James said, "Five o'clock tomorrow afternoon." Then Mr Turnip said something like, "You sure it will lift it? Remember the container will be heavy." I didn't hear the next bit because I had to order, but then Mrs Turnip asked why it had to be there exactly at five and James said, "Because everyone's rushing to get home and there's the handover to the night shift. The day shift are more likely to let us in because we're not going to be their problem and the night shift will assume it was fixed with the day shift and should be happy enough if we just do the job and clear off. So long as we don't make too much of a meal of it."'

She laughed. 'I only got all that because our first course arrived and you know what Mikolas is like, doesn't talk much when he eats. God knows how he ever chats anyone up. Maybe that's his problem. Part of it.'

'James Micklethwaite's like that. Says nothing at all until he's emptied his plate. So that was it? Nothing else?'

She stopped with her gin at her lips. 'What do mean? I'd like to see you—'

He held up his hands. 'All right, all right, I was just checking before we try to make sense of it.'

'There was a bit more, actually. Just before they left. I missed everything in between because Mikolas was going on about his bloody novel. But before they left – James left first, I think, he must have been standing up because I heard his chair and his voice was a bit clearer even though he was almost whispering – Mr Turnip said something like, "We'll be in the lay-by near the landfill site, so you'll have plenty of time. We'll be waiting for you." And James said, "It'll still be dark when we get to – to where we're going – in the morning. Why can't we just do it in the dark instead of hanging around until daylight? Much safer." And Mrs Turnip says, "These are orders, James. It has to be the right place for the right effect and it's more difficult to handle it and place it safely in the dark. We know how to handle it, we've got the gear and will do it as soon as it's light. Ten minutes later you'll be on your way home." There was something more but I didn't catch it.'

Charles sipped his whisky.

'It's clear they're nicking something,' she continued. 'But what, why and where are they taking it? And why do they need a crane? Any ideas, Mr Bond?'

Chapter Eighteen

The 1980s

Bob had rung Charles in the hotel first thing in the morning. 'I'm at home doing a ring-round of commercial vehicle-hire firms. Got a couple of calls to make as well. Meet me in my office soon as you can get back up here?'

Charles rang Sue's room. 'About to call Director K,' she said. 'Join you at breakfast. Start without me.'

They arrived at Northumbria Police HQ before Bob and had to wait at the entrance until his Sierra appeared. He signed them in and took them up to the Special Branch room, switching on the kettle as he entered without looking for the switch. 'No talk without caffeine. Should be some of yesterday's milk on the windowsill.' Once they were settled behind their mugs, he grinned. 'We've got him. At least, we've got what he's doing. It was the hire firm you mentioned, Charles, the one you saw the leaflet of in his flat. An Iveco truck with a tail-lift and forklift truck. Looks as if your theory might be right.'

'What theory?' asked Sue. 'You never said you had theories.'

'I don't very often. This one came on yesterday but it was a bit far-fetched and you'd have poured scorn all over me if we found he'd hired a normal car. The theory is Deep Blue. I think they're planning to grab it.'

'And do what?'

'Don't know.' He went to the large-scale map of the North East that covered most of one wall. 'Where's this Harlepool hire firm?'

Bob stood. 'The other way, towards the old quays. About there.' He put his finger on the map. Tell me again what Deep Blue is, exactly.'

Charles explained. Bob said, 'So, we've confirmed with the hire company that they're picking it up at five this afternoon and they're then RV-ing in a lay-by near the landfill site. Now, if my memory serves me well, that's on the way from the town to the power station.' He traced the route with his finger.

'Can we confirm whether the shift changes at five, as Sue heard?' asked Charles.

'Sure. But if what you say about this Deep Blue thing is right, I ought to brief the Assistant Chief Constable. And what could they do with it? Wouldn't be much use for blowing up King's Cross, would it? Assuming the IRA don't get there first. Unless they want to leave it on the concourse and irradiate a few hundred commuters.'

'We only know what Sue heard, which is that they want to take it somewhere where they'll arrive during the night and wait for dawn. The implication was that it's quite a distance, way off this map, I guess.'

There was a three-year-old AA atlas in the tea cupboard. Bob went off to the ACC's office, Sue took his place at his desk and rang her director. She broke off at one point, covering the receiver. 'He wants to know if you've kept Hookey informed and what is your theory about what they want it for.'

'Don't have one and haven't told Hookey yet. Trying to work out where they might be taking it.'

After she put the phone down, she said, 'He's going to get back to me with what he wants us to do. We've got to stay on this number until he does or let him know another. How's my Greek lover boy this morning?'

'On his way back to London, I hope.'

'Like he should've been last time.'

A few minutes later the phone rang. She answered it and held it out to Charles, eyebrows raised in warning.

'What the bloody hell are you doing up there, trying to start World War Three?'

Charles explained: 'I haven't been in touch because there was really nothing to report until now,' he concluded lamely.

'Stay where you are,' said Hookey, 'both of you, until I've spoken to Director K again.'

Bob returned, chastened. 'We've done it now. Soon

as I got there, the ACC had a call from your director, then he bollocked me for not telling him about it, then they got on to each other again on the Pickwick – you know, that secure phone that squawks – then I had to wait outside because there was something too hush-hush for me to know about, then I was summoned back in and told we've got to keep them all under twenty-four-hour surveillance and we can call on whatever resources we need – except that there aren't any because all our people are down in Manchester, helping out with a big IRA op – and then that they might send some of your people up from London but it'll be Christmas before they get here.' He grinned. 'Situation normal.'

Sue looked from one to the other. 'But just the three of us – how can they expect us – I mean, it takes dozens to do a proper surveillance job on just one—'

Charles held up the AA book. 'Mind if I hang on to this?'

That afternoon, Sue went with Bob in his car to the Melburys' hotel, where she waited in the car park while he went into the foyer to watch them out. Charles found the hire company in a corner of derelict land by the old quays and parked out of sight in a road of mostly boarded-up houses. He walked down to the water's edge, keeping the hire company in sight. The grey expanse of water was the only relief from general dilapidation.

Eventually, a brown Allegro turned into the hire company compound. Charles returned to his car and moved to within sight of the gates. It was some time before the blue Iveco truck hesitantly emerged and headed south towards the power station.

Driving a small lorry was obviously a novelty for James, whom Charles recalled as inept in practical things. Progress was slow and jerky, which made him difficult to follow without being spotted. Charles had to keep dropping back to let others pass and twice lost sight of the truck behind dust-carts. When James pulled into a filling station he continued some way past and pulled into a side road in case James had noticed the car. It was unlikely – handling the lorry probably took all his attention – but Charles also needed to find a call-box. The nearest one on the main road was out of order but he remembered seeing another just past the filling station and ran back, anxious to make the call and return to his car before James pulled past him again. The call-box was on the edge of what he had taken to be waste ground but which turned out to be the lay-by near the entrance to the landfill site, now seemingly an unofficial car park. As he picked up the receiver the Iveco pulled out of the filling station and immediately signalled left to turn in towards him. He turned his back to it as it pulled into the parking area and, after a five- or six-point turn, ended up facing him. He kept his back to it but could see it in the call-box mirror. Two figures emerged from among the parked cars, one carrying a holdall, and climbed into the truck's passenger door.

It pulled away as he dialled. There was no answer from Bob's office and Sue was not in her room at the hotel. He was running out of change but had just enough to ring the Office switchboard and ask them to pass his message for Sue to the MI5 switchboard. By the time he got back to his car the truck was out of sight.

This time James's slow progress was an advantage. The lorry was still on the A178 when he caught up with it and, by slip-streaming behind a recklessly driven Ford Transit, he was able to pass it and put some distance between it and him before the power station loomed like a sinister oversized blockhouse away to the left. By the time he took the turning towards it the day-shift early leavers were already coming out. Traffic both ways was delayed by an emerging low-loader bearing a large container. He was about to turn in when he spotted Bob's Sierra parked beyond the entrance.

'Jump in,' said Sue. 'We were just debating how long we were going to wait for you before going in ourselves.'

'Thought your people always had radios for jobs like this,' said Bob.

'They do but it wasn't meant to be a job like this

with just us and you.' She turned to Charles. 'Where is he? Have you seen him?'

'Him and them. They'll be here in minutes, we'd better get in there.'

Bob started the car. He didn't seem in any great hurry. 'We've got uniformed backup five minutes away in case there's any funny business.' He tapped his pocket. 'And I have got a radio. We're more sophisticated up North.'

He waved his police pass at the gatekeeper, who nodded him through. 'Couldn't even read it at that distance,' said Bob. 'Harder to get into Woolworths than here. Where now?'

'Up there, building on the left.' Charles pointed to the visitor centre, a portacabin at the foot of an array of high metal pipes belching steam.

Jackie, the guide, was wearing the grey trouser suit she'd had on before and was buttoning her coat. 'Hello, Mr Thoroughgood.' Her smile was as instant as before but she looked suddenly worried. 'Haven't forgotten an appointment, have I?'

'No, but we have a little business.' He motioned to Bob to show his pass. 'Deep Blue. We believe someone might be trying to steal it and we'd like you to get us in there so that we can speak to the staff.'

Jackie's eyes widened. 'Steal Deep Blue? Why would anyone want to? It would kill them. Anyway, it's not here any more.'

'Not here?'

'It's gone back to wherever they come from. It's at the end of its ... you know ... its half-life. There's a new one coming next week. They get replaced every so often.'

Bob smiled at her reassuringly. 'Like breeding bulls, eh?'

She laughed. 'That sort of thing, yes. They get used up.'

'When did it go?'

'I'm not sure, very recently, maybe today. Let me just ring down and see if there's anyone there.'

'If there is tell them we want to come down and see them.'

Eric, the man who had shown them Deep Blue, was waiting at the door of the concrete building. Charles noticed that the hoist pulley had moved. 'Too late, I'm afraid,' Eric said cheerfully. 'Just missed it. Went this afternoon. Not ten minutes ago. Tuesday next week, the new one comes. What's the rush, anyway?'

'Low-loader with a container?' asked Charles.

'White container, radiation markings on the sides. Did you see them? Not that that was it, not really. Deep Blue's in a small container inside that one, along with others, its little brothers and sisters. They pick them up from all over the place sometimes. Tons and tons of steel and concrete on that lorry, that's why it's a low-loader. What's your interest, anyway, gentlemen, if you don't mind my asking? Sorry, lady and gentlemen.'

'Here it is, they're coming,' said Sue.

The Iveco was just passing the raised barrier and turning down towards them. 'We'd better get inside out of sight,' Charles said to Eric. 'They know us.' Bob took out his radio.

'Who's coming, what's going on?' Charles heard him ask as he pulled the door to on himself and Sue.

Present Day

That was where Charles's file account ended. The rest of the file was a summary of what happened, added some time later by Sue. Neither she nor Charles witnessed anything from inside the bunker, nor could they influence what happened. Had it been his decision, Charles would not have allowed Bob to summon the two patrol cars and arrest James and the Melburys on grounds of conspiracy to commit robbery. He would have let them discover that Deep Blue was not there, follow them and see what they did next. Would they have tried to follow the low-loader and hijack it or would they have given up and tried again the following week with the new Deep Blue? Above all, he would have stayed his hand for as long as it took to get an idea of what they were intending to do with it. As it was, they never reached the bunker containing Deep Blue because James, turning too sharply, scraped the lorry along the side of one of the power-station vans. The damage was not serious and no one was hurt but the vocal disagreement that ensued provoked Bob to intervene and arrest them all.

The arrests came to nothing. Despite being held and questioned overnight none of them admitted to what they were trying to do and all three claimed that they had turned into the power station by mistake. The Melburys steadfastly offered no explanation for the protective clothing, with masks and gloves, in their holdall. They had clearly prepared for questioning and all three had agreed coordinated responses, based on knowledge of what the police were permitted to do by law. They refused to answer, as was their right, any questions about what they were doing together, how they knew each other, why they had hired the lorry, where they were going with it. James folded his arms, sat back and stared at the ceiling, while the Melburys said no more than that no one had committed any offence, which was true, and that they wished to go home, please.

James was released the following day but the Melburys were held for several more days while their immigration status was checked. Confronted with Canadian research into their passports and previous identities, they refused to respond, confident that there was no law against spying in Britain and that nothing could be done unless there was solid evidence that they had betrayed or sought to obtain classified information. They were confident, too, that the worst that could befall them was deportation. They had been well trained in taking advantage of liberal legal traditions.

They were duly deported after release without

charge, their real identities still unknown. They returned by circuitous route to the Soviet Union and, it was later learned, were awarded medals there and employed in training future Illegals.

Release, although it came sooner than for the Melburys, was not the end of the story for James. A search of his house yielded a small amount of cannabis and he was convicted of possession. That still annoyed him and, Charles assumed, probably accounted for the allegations in the *Sunday Times* that the authorities had sought to stifle Cold War protest by bringing unrelated minor criminal charges. He knew, too, that James suspected he was somehow responsible for his arrest, despite not having seen him and there being no evidence of a connection. He had overheard one of the policemen searching his house remark to a colleague that the cannabis find would make 'the Foreign Office bloke' happy. That, along with the coincidence of Charles's visit to retrieve his book, had confirmed his suspicion that he was under constant surveillance. 'He thinks that you personally are opening all his letters, listening to all his telephone calls, bugging his flat and making it difficult for him to get other teaching jobs,' Janet had guilelessly told Charles when they had run into each other again a year or so later. 'He blames you for everything that goes wrong with his life. As quite a lot does.'

Janet had laughed at that and Charles had smiled, acknowledging to himself that, for all its exaggeration and absurdity, James's paranoia had a grain of truth. And now, Charles mused as he closed the file, what he planned next would add a sack of grains.

Chapter Nineteen

The Present

Charles sat unmoving for a while after closing the file that evening. He was by no means the only late-stayer in the office – more people worked longer hours now, not always to commensurately greater effect – but he wished he were. It would have been appropriate to be alone because in closing the file he felt he was closing a chapter of his own youth. The image of Federov the survivor had stayed with him over the years; those thoughtful dark eyes, the heavy deliberate manner, the sense of hidden hinterland. His account of his return to the abandoned camp remained, for Charles, the key to the man. Federov's subsequent successes, the compromises he must have made, the betrayals, the switched loyalties, getting himself accepted by the Party and his subsequent pursuit of ascendency, he must have justified to himself by reference to his time in the camp: 'I was here.' The system that had done this to him deserved no loyalty, he would have told himself.

Provided, that is, he had felt the need for justification at all. Charles suspected he had too sentimental a view of the man. After all, he had secured his heart surgery in London and then returned to Moscow where he lived for another year before suffering a stroke, without re-emerging to repay the debt he had promised. The only information he had given was the cryptic reference to Deep Blue and that had proven inconclusive. When the case was closed it was not as a failed but as an undeveloped case, unlikely ever to be reopened. Except that Charles had reopened it, though even now he couldn't be sure that his attempt to give it posthumous value wasn't wishful thinking.

He had to wait until dinner with Sarah that night to hear more about the current Deep Blue.

'You know I offloaded that Triple A case to Timothy and his merry men,' she said. 'Boys and girls, I should say. Well, I was seeing him about something else today and couldn't help noticing a reference to Deep Blue on his screen. Of course, I shouldn't be telling you this, serious breach of professional etiquette and client confidentiality. You won't tell anyone, will you?'

Charles poured more wine.

'We really should eat better,' she continued. 'That's the second time this week you've had pizza. I'm proving a rotten wife, aren't I? Don't say you weren't warned.'

'I thought you were about to demonstrate what a good one you are.'

'Spy, not wife. Much easier.' She sipped her wine. 'What I saw was a summary of a case conference, not all of it. Done by one of Timothy's juniors, I should think. It referred directly to Deep Blue, which is what caught my eye. Though it only gave that name in brackets, "often referred to as". I think its technical designation must have been on the previous page. Anyway, it appeared to be a commentary on or summary of a case Triple A wants to make on health and safety grounds – those two dear friends of the legal profession – to have Deep Blue removed from the industrial estate just outside Newcastle where I told you it now lives. They claim it's too easily accessed and is vulnerable to terrorist hijack, without saying what terrorists would do with it if it didn't kill them in the process of taking it. They've got the local MP involved, too. You know what it's like with anything radioactive – mention the word and everyone goes into spasm. It's not much of a case, from what I could see, just an excuse to make trouble and draw attention to themselves. Coincides with the forthcoming riot – sorry, rally – they're planning in Trafalgar Square.'

'How soon is that?'

'Next Saturday. You should pay more attention to the news and less to all your secret stuff. Actually, I got the impression from Timothy that this case is really just a dry run for the removal of the nuclear submarines from Faslane and Coulport. At least they're going the legal route.'

ALAN JUDD

'Unless it's a twin-track approach like the old IRA one – bullet and ballot box.'

She sighed. 'When I was growing up in North-umberland we had a Jack Russell like you. Ben. Whenever he found a rat-hole he'd dig away at it for days, long after all the rats had fled, barking, barking, barking. Used to drive my mother mad. You really think that, at the same time as taking legal action to move Deep Blue, Triple A would be so daft as to pinch it? I know you don't think much of what your friend James thinks, but he's not actually that stupid, is he?'

'He's bright but he's bitter and his judgement's always been a bit iffy. He's capable of it.' He went through his theory again.

She shook her head. 'All very interesting, Mr Thoroughgood, but what this court wants to hear is evidence and all you have produced is supposition and theory, as your MI5 man said. You've lined up your ducks in a row but they're all your own ducks, they're not evidence independent of you. Maybe you're right that James is daft enough to want to repeat what he failed to achieve years ago, but how does that fit with the strategy of the organisation of which he's a prom-inent part and what on earth do they think they're going to do with Deep Blue when they get it? They're not terrorists intent on mass murder, as you admit yourself.'

'Some – a few – may be. We don't know. It only

takes one or two. As for strategy, a secret twin-track approach would make sense from their point of view. Call it surface fleets and submarines, to make it more topical. The surface fleet is the legal case and Trafalgar Square demos and all that public sort of thing, the submarine fleet is direct action to spread panic, confusion and recrimination. I'd certainly consider that if I were them.' He had always enjoyed gaming the opposition, whether states or terrorists. It was fun and usually left the gamer – aware of the weaknesses of his own side – feeling he could achieve far more than the opposition, if only he were that way inclined. 'Or maybe it's just that James and his Rob S. Ready friend – whoever he is – are part of a maverick group operating unknown to the rest. You could see their reasoning, either way. But working out what they intend to do with it when they get it is another matter.'

This time she poured the wine. 'I'll tell you what I'd do.'

The next morning, Charles rang Simon Mall on the secure phone. Neither had time to meet and the call was shorter than Charles would have liked but, in view of what he planned, he felt he owed it to Simon to give him one more chance to act. He outlined his thinking, as before, adding Sarah's theory about the possible use of Deep Blue. 'It fits with what the Russians might have done with it when they tried to pinch it during the Cold War,' he concluded. 'Not to mention James's involvement both times. That can't be coincidence and he must be itching to make up for his cock-up last time.'

Simon's pause was long enough for Charles to imagine his expression. 'Let me run that back past you to check I've got it right,' said Simon. 'Your pair of mavericks break in and steal Deep Blue, with or without the knowledge of the rest of Triple A. They don't, as terrorists might, take it to a football stadium and kill thousands or leave it on a commuter train. Instead, they then take it to the nuclear submarine base on Faslane, or the Coulport weapons arsenal in nearby Loch Long, and drop it in the water and kill all the fish. That's what you're saying?'

'Maybe not *all* the fish, because I'm told alpha radiation doesn't travel far in water, which is why it's kept in a well. But enough fish to be noticed and cause panic. Alternatively, they could put it on land in or near the base where it would presumably kill any vegetation or animals or people within range. But that would include them unless they've worked out a way of not exposing themselves. So it's more likely they'll dump it in the loch.'

'But why? I can see it would cause some trouble but it's not going to do any real harm, unlike a mass-casualty attack.'

Despite his bureaucratic caution, Simon Mall was in some ways a political innocent. Charles chose his words carefully, beginning with the opposite of what he meant. 'You're right, of course, it would be nothing like as deadly as a mass-casualty attack. But at the same time it would be more than just "some trouble". It would be a media sensation, a gift to the anti-nuclear movement and a powerful political weapon for the SNP, who want Trident out of Scotland. Everyone would assume it was the nuclear subs or their missiles that had caused the radiation deaths and it could easily become politically impossible to resist SNP demands to move them. And perhaps politically difficult to find an alternative home for Trident, because although you can apparently tell very quickly that it's the wrong kind of radiation to have come from the subs or missiles, government denials would never be believed. The damage would be done.'

There was a pause. 'How sure are you that dumping Deep Blue in the loch would have such an effect?'

'Almost certain, but it's being confirmed now.' Charles exaggerated – he had asked Elaine to ask the MI6 counter-proliferation team but hadn't heard back. 'The thing is, it's essentially a political act, intended to bring about a political change and not done with the intention of killing people, though it may have that result. Still a criminal act, of course, and probably falling under the Terrorism Act, which would mean you're entitled to investigate it.'

There was another pause. He could sense Simon's sceptical smile. 'Ingenious idea, Charles. Come up with it yourself?'

To say that his wife had suggested it over dinner and a little too much wine was unlikely to convince. 'I was persuaded of it by looking at the old case when James tried it before and adding that to what we know now about his involvement with Triple A and rumours of direct action.'

'Seem, might, may, could – it's all hypothesis. We have no actual evidence that this is what they're planning.'

'You haven't looked for it.'

'Hard to mount an investigation of this sort without informing Melanie or without her finding out about it. Also hard to believe she doesn't know about it given that she lives with James. And if she does she'd surely try to stop it, given her closeness – former closeness – to the Home Secretary. If we investigated without telling her and she found out—'

'But it must be possible. Give it a nickname and pretend it's something else.'

Someone interrupted Simon. When he came back he said, 'Sorry, I've got a meeting. Interesting theory, Charles. I'll think about it. We should discuss it again.'

'Of course, they might be planning a mass-casualty attack after all.' Charles threw that in just before the line went dead. He didn't believe it, didn't believe that James would intend mass murder. Sarah's Faslane theory was more plausible, and cleverer. But nor did he trust James's judgement. Simon had responded much as he had anticipated – no commitment and the usual reluctance to investigate. He had done what he could to interest those who ought to be interested, so half his cover for his own action was in place.

'No problems, Charles, we can fix that, I'm sure.' Robin Cleveley sounded pleased to be consulted. 'She's in Brussels this afternoon, flying back this evening, coming straight back to the office, of course. No surprise there. I'll get something in the diary and ring you back with the time. Great to speak.'

Charles replaced the receiver with a wince, only then realising that Elaine was standing in his office door, observing. 'I can usually tell who you're talking to by your face. One of the SPADS?'

'You'd think after decades of secret service on behalf of Her Majesty I might have learned to dissemble better.'

'Well, I've got some answers to your questions about radiation from the counter-proliferation people so you can practise being an expert on that. Or would you rather they came and briefed you themselves?'

'I might. Let me see.'

The notes had what he needed.

Early that evening he was in the Foreign Secretary's large corner office overlooking Downing Street and St James's Park. Robin was there along with Elspeth Jones's private secretary, a thin, earnest, bespectacled young man of a type often found in Whitehall private offices, meticulously efficient and possessed of tenacious memory.

His presence was initially queried by Robin, who turned to the Foreign Secretary. 'I'm not sure whether Alasdair—'

'I think he should stay,' said Charles. 'No need to be off-record.' The Foreign Secretary looked momentarily taken aback at the intervention but Charles reckoned it worth the risk. He wanted a meticulous record.

The Foreign Secretary flopped into one of the leather armchairs, waving the others to do the same. She looked tired but her manner was businesslike. 'Charles, you're hoping I can give you a date for your move from Croydon. I'm afraid I can't. In fact, it's worse than that. Government policy, as you know, is wherever possible to move departments out of central London, so moving one back in would be hard to justify no matter what assurances my predecessor gave. On top of that, the Chancellor announced at Cabinet yesterday that he's going to ask all departments to freeze office moves for the rest of this financial year at least and probably for the next. Austerity bites on.' Her smile was brief and wintry. 'So no moves at all. Sorry about that.'

'Thank you, Secretary of State. It's helpful to know we won't be packing our toothbrushes just yet. But it wasn't that that I asked to see you about. I want to discuss something that Robin and I have been following for a while now with growing unease.' He told her everything, including Simon Mall's reaction and exaggerating only Robin's role, relying on the flattery of inclusion to secure his agreement. Robin nodded.

When he had finished Elspeth Jones sighed and looked down at her hands clasped upon her lap. 'So are you saying that the SNP might be party to this Triple A plan in the same way that they're supporting the Trafalgar Square rally?'

'I don't know, they could be. Probably not. The only link with them is the involvement of this SNP renegade. We don't even know for certain that Triple A itself is behind it. What we do know is that two people associated with both organisations seem to be involved in it.'

'It. Whatever "it" is. If it exists. It's no more than your own unproven hypothesis at the moment.'

'But we do know that one of the same people tried it before.'

She picked at something on her dark skirt and flicked it to the floor. 'Do you think those involved include the Home Secretary's SPAD, this Melanie ...'

'Stokes,' said Robin. 'Melanie Stokes. It's hard to believe she knows nothing, despite what she said to Charles. Given who she lives with. And if she knows then presumably the Home Secretary ...'

Elspeth glanced sharply at him. 'There's no indication that he knows anything of this?'

'Not yet.'

She continued to look interrogatively at Robin, then gave another cool smile. 'Mind you, he's privately no friend to Trident so it probably wouldn't break his heart if it were moved or dismantled as a result of overwhelming public protest. But there are a lot of ifs in this.' She looked back at Charles. 'What are you asking? Are you suggesting we should be doing something about it and, if so, what?'

'I'm suggesting what I suggested to the DDG of MI5: that we should take action to find out whether they're doing what I suspect, at the same time taking steps to ensure that Deep Blue is safe. That would mean putting the suspected conspirators under surveillance and moving or guarding Deep Blue.'

'You know very well I have no power to authorise surveillance of British subjects in the UK. That's very much the Home Secretary's prerogative and he's hardly likely to agree a warrant application from you which is not supported by MI5.'

'I think the relevant legislation specifies authorisation by the Secretary of State, without saying *which* secretary of state, you or the Home Secretary. So technically you could.' He knew it was a hopeless case but he wasn't making it with any expectation of winning. Out of the corner of his eye he could see Alasdair assiduously noting the exchange, which was what he wanted. 'Or you could of course ask the Prime Minister to put pressure on the Home Secretary.'

Elspeth looked at him as if suspecting he wasn't

serious, then ignored his point. 'Who owns Deep Blue, anyway?'

The question hadn't occurred to Charles. 'I don't know. The Department of Business and Skills? The Atomic Energy Authority? Some private—'

'I suggest you start by finding out and then tell them your theory. Then it'll be up to them to ensure its safety and you'll have done all you reasonably and legally can.'

She was right. That would of course be the sensible thing to do. As often with sensible things, it was less appealing than the alternative. Charles nodded. 'Thank you, Secretary of State.'

Afterwards he and Robin meditatively descended the grand staircase, Charles running his hand down the wide banister. 'Frankly,' said Robin, 'I think that went about as badly as it could have.'

'In one sense, yes.'

'In what sense didn't it?'

Charles hesitated. It could be useful to involve Robin, but he was Elspeth's creature and his loyalty, such as it was, would always be to her. He decided against it. 'Of course, I should have mugged up on who owns Deep Blue.'

Robin said nothing as they turned the corner of the stairs and a couple of young men hurried past, laughing. Then Robin stopped. 'Between ourselves – strictly between ourselves – I'm as frustrated about this as you are and equally convinced there's something

serious going on. I've got a friend who works for ...
well, in the software industry, in a company – and he's
found out a bit more about Rob S. Ready and your
friend James. Ready's been doing Google searches of
an industrial estate in Newcastle and James has been
taking HGV driving lessons. They've also been talking
dates. Haven't told Elspeth because what my friend's
doing may not be completely legal and she'd run a mile
at that.'

'Which dates?'

'I don't know. He just told me this on the phone. I
stopped him going into more detail.'

'Is it seriously illegal?'

'I'm not sure, rather not know; I haven't asked how
he does it. His company wouldn't be pleased, I'm sure
of that.'

'If he's doing it at your request it probably is illegal.'

Robin nodded. His expression was always sharp
and alert, a fox on scent, his eye to his own advantage. But he seemed committed to this issue, perhaps
through rivalry with Melanie Stokes. He could be –
was being – useful. Charles changed his mind. 'Let
me explain why, from my point of view, the exchange
with the Foreign Secretary went well. And how you
can help, if you will. But this has, as you said, to be
strictly between ourselves.'

They both knew that stock phrases of assurance,
along with others such as 'within these four walls',
'between you, me and the gatepost' and 'keep it under

your hat', were breached as often as they were given. Secrets were part of the currency of bureaucratic life, there to be traded. The only way to keep them was not to tell them until they rusted, when no one was interested. But the ritual of assurance was still useful because it gave the confider the weapon of blame, if required.

Two more people passed them on the stairs. 'Let's discuss it outside,' said Charles. They spent about ten minutes in the quadrangle, sheltering behind government delivery vans from buffeting gusts of wind and rain. Robin was enthusiastic. 'Always longed to do a bit of secret squirrel stuff.'

'Just keep it to yourself.'

'Of course, of course.'

Chapter Twenty

The Present

Sarah was not pleased when he rang with his suggestion. 'What, after they leaked all that stuff to the press after last time? We don't owe them anything after that. Anyway, we saw them only the week before last and I don't think I could trust myself not to give them both a piece of my mind.'

'I suspect it was James's doing and that she's embarrassed about it.'

'What difference does that make? She should have stopped him.'

'But it's not for social reasons. It's to try to find out more about what he's planning, whether your suggestion is right.'

'Can't you find that out some other way? You ought to be in a position to. It's ridiculous to say we have to have them for dinner.'

'I'm being blocked by MI5.'

They went on for a few minutes more until eventually

she sighed and said, 'Well, there's nothing in the house as you know and I haven't time to go shopping.'

'I'll get some ready-cooked stuff.'

'We can't do that when we're inviting people to dinner.'

'They didn't even bother with that. They took us out. We never got to their place.'

She sighed again. 'I'll get something on the way home. Not that I don't trust your choice, of course.'

'I owe you one.'

'You owe me masses.'

There was more truth in that than she might have intended. 'Are you beginning to regret marrying me?'

'Not quite. But you're getting close to the edge.'

Melanie sounded pleased when he rang her. They would love to, it would be wonderful to come to dinner and see their new house. She would have to check with James but she was sure it would be all right.

They turned up punctually. Melanie extravagantly admired the house and gushed over Sarah's announcement of shepherd's pie, which Sarah did not confess was bought. James, silent until prompted by Melanie, feigned an interest in their new radiators.

'I've some news for you,' Charles said to Melanie as he poured the wine.

She pulled a face. 'Don't tell me. You've snatched

Victoria Street from our jaws. That's why you're being so nice.'

'Quite the opposite. We've changed our minds, told the Cabinet Office we'll put up with Croydon for the time being. My board feels a move would be too disruptive at the moment. I agreed. So it's all yours. Assuming you can persuade the powers that be.' He ignored Sarah's surprised interrogative glance.

The lie proved fecund. Melanie's brittle eagerness to please was replaced by a more relaxed sociability, enough for her to resume her conversation with Sarah about the legal profession without too obviously listening for anything Charles might say. He tried to engage James on recent opinion polls which contradicted each other on public attitudes to government spending, probably reflecting the attitudes of those who commissioned them. James's responses were monosyllabic and he seemed reluctant to meet Charles's eye. That was fine so far as Charles was concerned, since his target was Melanie. He turned to her and said, 'We must be about due another tripartite, aren't we?' When she looked puzzled, as he anticipated, he explained that these were regular meetings between the heads of MI5, MI6 and GCHQ to ensure cooperation and to agree lines to take with Whitehall and the Treasury. 'Up to you whether MI5 is represented by you or Simon Mall but it would be sensible to talk soon before the budget negotiations. How's your programme over the next couple of weeks?'

She took her phone from her handbag, cited some dates the following week, then retracted. 'Oh no, we're away on a midweek break, aren't we?' She glanced at James.

'Only me,' he said promptly. 'I'm on that conference.'

'The conference, of course. I was muddling this month with next. So, no, yes, I am free then.'

'I'll ask my secretary to get in touch with yours,' said Charles. The three days of James's alleged conference were, he saw, the three before Triple A's Trafalgar Square rally.

'Midweek breaks are such a good idea,' said Sarah. 'We went to Salzburg before Christmas. The benefit lasts much longer than the break itself.'

Later, when Melanie went to the loo, Charles prepared coffee in the kitchen. She stopped on her way back. 'Nice to see your domestic skills on display.'

'I'm pretty hot at putting cups on a tray.'

She indicated the coffee machine. 'Are they any good, these things? I was wondering about getting one.'

'Wait and see. I'm not sure it's ever hot enough.' He folded his arms and stood leaning against the sink. 'Tell me, you and the Home Secretary – I mean, it's common knowledge that you and he were once ... does it make your professional relationship easier or more difficult?'

The question caught her off guard but she managed a smile. 'Well, I'm not sure it's that common, is it? More so than I thought, obviously. But, no, it's not a problem. I don't think it makes much difference either way.' She folded her arms too, pushing up her breasts and leaning against the kitchen cupboard opposite him. 'After all, we're all grown-ups, aren't we?' She smiled.

Charles turned to attend to the coffee. People felt less like cornered interviewees if you seemed otherwise engaged while questioning them. 'Presumably it makes it easier if he trusts you to know his mind on things without having to go to him about everything you're doing.'

'I suppose so. He leaves me a pretty free hand, but I still make sure he knows what I'm doing.'

Charles looked at her now, raising his eyebrows. 'Everything?'

She raised her own eyebrows. 'So far.'

Flirtation, now that he was married, felt like adultery, though that was not his motive. 'He doesn't worry about you and James? I don't mean personally but politically, given James's . . .'

She shook her head. 'He knows I play no part in what James does. Or writes. Not that he necessarily disagrees with it. They coincide on some issues.'

'He's not worried about being damaged by association?'

She looked down at her feet. She wore black boots with moderately high heels, her blue jeans tucked into them. Her arms were still folded. She looked up again. 'The thing is, with me and James, it's been a long time. Things change over the years. I don't see it as a permanent fixture.'

'Are you all right with the coffee?' Sarah stood in the door.

'Just coming.' Charles handed the loaded tray to Melanie. 'You take that and I'll pour.'

In the hall, when they were leaving, he said to James, 'How many are you expecting?' James looked non-plussed. 'At the rally.'

'Oh, the demo, yes. Forty to fifty thousand.'

'See you there.'

James looked puzzled again until he saw that Charles was smiling. 'Don't bet on it.'

'Will you be speaking?'

'Not this time.'

'But you'll be there?'

'If I can.'

When the door was closed on them and their foot-steps had faded Sarah threw the tea-towel at him. 'Your turn. I want a leisurely bath. Talk about sticky, he could barely bring himself to speak to me in there while you and Melanie were in the kitchen. In the end I stopped trying. At least he won't have any gossip to leak to the *Sunday Times* this time. What were you two talking about, anyway?'

'Trying to gauge where her loyalties lie and whether she and the Home Secretary have any idea of what might be going on.'

'And did she tell you?'

'Not in so many words. But the evening told us that James will be away the three days running up to the rally, just when you'd expect him to be fully focused on it, which suggests to me they're planning their spectacular to coincide with it. It was clear, too, from that last exchange, that his mind isn't on the rally at all. And Melanie made it sound as if the Home Secretary isn't entirely unsympathetic to at least some of James's aims. Doesn't mean he knows what James is planning, of course. Nor she. My guess, given what she's said before, is she doesn't know about it.'

'But there isn't an *it*, Charles. There's only my theory which happens to coincide with what they might have tried and failed to do years ago. You don't actually *know* anything, except that they seem to be planning to do something with this Deep Blue thing.'

'That's what we find out next, I hope.'

She paused on the stairs. 'We?'

'Faslane was your idea. The more I think about it, the more likely it seems. You'd want to be in on it, wouldn't you? See yourself triumphantly proven right. If you can get leave.'

'Get on with the washing up.'

Charles's contacts with Robin over the next few days were more frequent than Charles would have liked and hard to regulate, with Robin becoming ever more excited through texts and calls. They had one

ALAN JUDD

face-to-face meeting, unavoidably in Charles's club.

'We've got them now,' said Robin in dramatic under-
tone as they took their drinks to a corner. 'They're
driving up to Newcastle in James's car on Sunday and
staying in some place belonging to someone Ready
knows. That is his real name, by the way, Rob S.
Ready. Not clear when they're planning to be back.'

Charles's mind was half on possible consequences.
'This is through your software contact acting illegally?'

Robin held up both hands. 'Did I say that? Did he
tell me he is? I ask him things and he tells me. I don't
ask how he finds out.'

'I doubt that's a defence, but go on.'

'Well, that's it. Except they're taking a lot of cash
with them. Five grand. No mention of why. So how
are we going to keep tabs on them when we get there
if we don't know where they're going to be?'

'There's someone up there who might be able to
help us.'

'I still don't quite understand why you can't use your
own people. You must have people trained to do this
sort of thing.'

'I'm trying not to use Office resources, as I said
before. Partly because it couldn't be done officially
without risking Melanie finding out, partly because
it's not our patch but MI5's and they're not keen, and
partly because if it all goes pear-shaped there's less
splash-back on my Service. It's me that would take
the blame.'

'And this wonderful establishment, your club, where the dastardly deed was planned. Better put me up before it happens.'

The next morning, Charles rang Bob Shea, now head of Northumbria Special Branch. 'A blast from the past,' he said, introducing himself. 'We haven't spoken this century. I don't know whether you remember our wild goose chase—'

Bob remembered, laughing. 'And your colleague, that nice ...'

'Sue, still around, still working. Married now – or again, rather – with children. Sends her best.'

'Have a lot more to do with her office now than we used to, all this terrorism stuff. They're even embedded with us sometimes. Makes life interesting. What can I do for you? Not still chasing after Deep Blue, are you?'

'Something like that.' Charles outlined the story and his theory. 'I'll give you chapter and verse when we come up, including why we're going about it in this slightly unconventional way.'

'I'm all for that. Bit of fun does us all good.'

Chapter Twenty-One

The Present

The red-brick terraced cottage in Carlisle was superficially as neat and inconspicuous as its neighbours, with its black front door, white window frames, grey slate roof, two-pot chimney and lop-sided television aerial. Closer inspection, however, would have shown the door-paint beginning to peel, some rot in the window frames and the once-white windowsills a dirty grey. There were faded net curtains on all the windows.

The neighbours knew it as a rented house occupied in quick succession by tenants who were part of a large, amorphous, itinerant, youthful urban population. In the past two years the oldest and longest-lasting had been a woman in her thirties with three young children. She was there about ten months before disappearing overnight. The house was then given over to builders and decorators for a few weeks before two women in their twenties moved in. After a month or so they were joined by a man who left a fortnight later with one of the women, the other staying for another month. Next came a young man who was rarely seen or heard except late at night when he played loud music. He would turn it off after threats from neighbours but would start again a few nights later. After six months the police came at six o'clock one morning and took him away. The house was said to be owned by a landlord who had many such properties and lived in Keswick.

The latest tenant was another young man, a quieter one who played no loud music, slept at night and went to work during the day. No one knew what he did but his hours were long and it was often late evening before his ten-year-old Nissan Micra returned to the street. He was overweight, sometimes wore grey tracksuit trousers instead of jeans, shaved infrequently and bought his meals at the nearby Turkish takeaway. He told a neighbour his name was Zac.

During the evening before Charles and Sarah travelled north two visitors arrived to stay with Zac. One was James and the other his friend, Rob. They arrived in James's Toyota from which Rob, tall and gangling with shoulder-length brown hair, took time to unfold himself. Straightened, he looked up and down the quiet street, whooped loudly, then grinned at James. 'That'll wake 'em up, the buggers.' His accent was Glaswegian. He shouldered his sleeping bag and rucksack. James looked disapproving but said nothing.

Later, amid the detritus of kebabs and cans of beer, the three of them sat in the small living room. Rob was on the floor, his back against the wall, smoking roll-ups and using an empty beer can as an ashtray. Zac slumped on the sagging sofa, drinking. James sat at the small folding table near the window, with a notebook. The atmosphere was tense.

'It's not as complicated as it sounds,' James said quietly, looking at Zac. 'You pick it up as arranged, all official and above board. You set off back towards Sellafield—'

'He's crapping himself, got the trots about it, haven't you, Zac? Eh? Smell him from here,' said Rob.

James ignored him. 'You stop at the Little Chef after Hexham on the A69 because you need a leak or a cuppa or because you're tired or your tachometer shows you're running close to your hours. Whatever suits. You often stop there, that's your story, remember, whenever you're moving stuff that way. And you park in the corner by the hedge and trees, nose in as close to the hedge and trees as you can get. There's a wastebin there, you can't miss it. You go in and get a cup of tea or have a pee or whatever—'

'Half a dozen cream buns, more like,' said Rob.

'. . . leaving the cab unlocked. Important, that, because we'll be in the trees and we'll climb in when no one's around and you're having your pee.'

'Where will you park?' asked Zac.

'Other side of the road in the Henshaw service

station, in the MOT bit. We've actually booked it in for one. Better bloody pass. Don't want a wasted journey, do we, Zac?' James smiled as if encouraging a child. Zac remained slumped over his beer can, mouth open, looking at him. 'Then we drive off to where we're going, you keeping your head down out of sight with us in the cab until we're clear. When we get there Rob and I unload it, no danger to you or us, then we drive back, tie you up in the back of the lorry – empty now, remember – in such a way that you can get free after a while, and then you call the police and tell them two blokes jumped you when you went to get back in the cab, drove for miles, stopped and unloaded it, God knows where or into what – you were blindfolded – then drove back and left you. Never said a word to you apart from keep still and you'll be all right. OK, Zac?'

'When do I get paid?' He had a squeaky, incipiently resentful voice.

'Half now and half when we get back.'

'Where?'

'In the lorry. We won't come back here, to your home.'

'What if the police find all that cash when they search the lorry?'

James glanced at Rob and raised his eyebrows, but Rob merely shrugged. 'Stick it in your wallet,' said James. 'They probably won't search you but if they do just say you're looking to buy another car and you always get them cheaper with cash.'

'And will I, you know – it's dangerous, all this radiation, that's why it's in that heavy container – stop it leaking? When you take it out, how do we know we won't all get . . . ?'

'Zapped? Fried to cinders? Good thinking, Zac. Hadn't thought of that.' Rob laughed.

'Don't worry about the radiation,' said James. 'That's all taken into account. For one thing, it's at the end of its half-life so it's nothing like as powerful as it was, which is why it's being replaced. For another, all the time you're in the lorry it'll be in its container, so you're perfectly safe. It'll still be in its container when we get it out and lower it into the water, where it's also safe so long as you don't get too close, go swimming round it or anything daft like that. Then we release it from the container and drive off. All it's going to do is kill a few hundred fish through its natural toxicity, which is all we need it to do to make everyone think it's the nuclear submarines and their missiles leaking radiation.'

'And then there'll be such a bloody great outcry,' said Rob, 'they'll have to move the whole lot out o' Sco'land and take them down south where they can bloody keep them if they want.'

'Which they won't, so they'll have to get rid of them altogether and we'll have a nuclear-free Britain without anyone being hurt or harmed except a few fish,' said James.

'And independence for Sco'land. Irresistible,' said Rob.

Zac seemed unmoved. 'What if the police don't believe me?'

'Why shouldn't they?' said James. 'They can't prove anything. All you have to do is stick to your story and they have to let you go.'

'What if I get the sack?'

'You won't. They can't, not under modern employment law if it's not your fault.'

'But if they did who's gonna find me another job?'

'We'll see you all right, Zac,' said Rob, quietly now. 'Dinna worry y'sel'.'

Chapter Twenty-Two

The Present

Bob Shea had gained weight and lost hair during the years since he and Charles had last met. He had transferred to Northumbria Police and his office was still in the detached inter-war house at police headquarters outside Newcastle, albeit that he now had a room to himself.

He shook hands with Sarah. 'Hope he's not dragged you out on a wild-goose chase like the last time he was in this part of the world.'

'He didn't need to drag me. I'm combining this with a visit to my mother in Hexham.'

'At least he's had the good sense to marry a local girl. I don't have to call him sir, then.' He chuckled.

Over tea, Charles explained their visit, neglecting only to mention that Robin Cleveley had accompanied them. Bob's round, good-natured face looked perplexed. 'Well, I can see why the DDG might be cautious about committing resources, given he's got this female political commissar looking over his shoulder. But I don't see why he couldn't have picked up the phone to us. We could check things out, make sure everything's OK, keep tabs on James Micklethwaite for him. Must say I wouldn't mind a chance to feel James's collar again. He's got no better as he's got older, then?'

His phone rang. He listened for a minute or so, said he'd ring back on another line, excused himself and left the office. When he returned he looked more serious. 'Charles, it seems to me the best thing would be to make sure we've got each other's numbers and for me to know where you're staying and that sort of thing, and for you to keep me in touch with what you're doing, what you're planning. I'll get someone to check out Deep Blue in the meantime and keep an eye out for young – not so young now, is he? – James and his oppo, Rob Roy or whatever he calls himself. See if we've got anything on him. So all you need do is sit tight and I'll let you know if anything comes up.'

Afterwards, as they drove away, Sarah said, 'What do you think that was all about, that call he took? His manner was quite different afterwards, much less relaxed and helpful, quite apart from saying "don't call us, we'll call you".'

'He didn't actually say that.'

'As good as. I think he's been warned off you.'

Charles thought so too but didn't like to admit it. 'We'll manage without him, then.'

They and Robin, who had come by train, were

booked into a hotel on the rebuilt waterfront, over-looking the Tyne's famous bridges. It was expensive and hardly inconspicuous but Charles had insisted on somewhere with safe garaging for his Bristol. It was also, he argued, a part of town unlikely to be visited by James and Rob S. Ready.

'Presumably the Office is paying for us and Robin?' asked Sarah.

'Only if I turn out to be right.'

'And if not?'

'I guess I pay. I'm on leave, remember. Same as you. No win, no fee. Now commonplace in your profession.'

She looked at the bleak housing estate by the side of the dual carriageway. 'That's usually based on a rather more precise estimate of probability.'

Robin was having coffee and biscuits in the lounge. 'Sorry, couldn't wait for lunch.' He kissed Sarah as if they were old friends. 'Join me while we sort out a POA?' He smiled at Charles. 'Plan of action.'

Coffee and cake were tempting. They sat, and Charles told him what Bob had said. 'But I don't think we should hang around waiting to hear if anyone else does anything,' he concluded. 'We should act.'

Robin grinned, the last piece of cake still in his mouth. 'All for that. All for action.'

'We'll drive out to the industrial estate where Deep Blue is now kept and talk to the people who guard or look after it.'

'Saying what – that it may be about to be hijacked?'

'Perhaps not in quite so many words ...'

'Hard to think what others you could use,' said Sarah. 'What else have you got to talk to them about? And who will you say you are, anyway? You can't say you're the Chief of MI6, unless you want it splashed all over the evening news. Even if you did, what locus do you have, what business is it of yours? It's a police matter, surely, and they now know about it.'

'A lawyer speaks.' Charles smiled but she had a point. He had assumed anything he did would be in conjunction with Special Branch, which would have given him – all three of them – the cover of anonymity at least.

'And the law will want answers if you're caught trying to pass yourself off as someone else while on leave and interfering with what should be someone else's official business. Not to mention the media.'

'Use me,' said Robin. He waved to the waitress for more coffee. 'I could be an investigative journalist looking into nuclear and radiological storage issues.'

'Working for whom?'

'Freelance.'

'Where has your stuff appeared? Where's your Facebook page? Why aren't you on LinkedIn? What happens if they Google you?'

'Pity, I always rather fancied journalism. I'll be a businessman, then. Possible client. I may want to use Deep Blue for cleaning ... I don't know, artificial hips.'

Sarah laughed. 'For re-use?'

'Only in China.'

'Company name, business cards, website?' said Charles.

Robin held up his hands. 'Oh, all right, Nuclear Safety Inspectorate. Snap inspection.'

'Getting there,' said Charles. 'But you've no telephone number or anything like that.'

'You could fix that, surely? You must have lots of disposable numbers. Oh no, sorry, we're not allowed official facilities, are we?'

Charles put his hands palms down on the coffee table. 'The best lies are closest to the truth. You are who you are, own name, we're long-suffering friends you're staying with nearby, no need for our names. You're researching a book on peaceful nuclear power, have heard about Deep Blue and wanted to check that it is what you think it is and if possible see it in action. In the course of conversation you express concern about security, which, at the very least, might remind them of it and make them more watchful. We, meanwhile, will be discreetly recce-ing the surroundings for anywhere we can hide and watch to see if James and co. try to hijack it again. They've got a pretty small time window, essentially today and tonight, if they want news of it to coincide with tomorrow's Trafalgar Square demo. So we shouldn't have to wait long.'

'I'll go and change,' said Robin. 'Look less like a city slicker, more like a dotty author.'

When he had gone Sarah said, 'You're not seriously

thinking we'll hang around all day watching the place, are you?'

'Not all of us, just me. If I can find a dustbin to hide in.'

She looked at him. 'You know I normally trust your judgement but this time I'm beginning to—'

'It's not just me. Robin seems pretty convinced.'

'Only because he romanticises the intelligence world. He'd soon change his tune if he thought this would make the Foreign Secretary look bad rather than the Home Secretary.'

'Yes, you can't trust him.'

She smiled. 'Maybe not, but he's rather charming.'

It was not hard to find the industrial estate, which they had seen signposted on the way into the city. Robin, folded into the back of the Bristol despite Sarah's protestations, seemed more interested in asking Charles about the car than in what they were doing. 'You need to focus on what you're going to say,' said Charles. 'Rehearse it now.' There was plenty of time as they were soon lost in the industrial estate, which appeared to have more to do with storage than industry and in which the buildings, all numbered units, looked alike.

'God-forsaken place,' said Robin. 'What do people do here?'

'They're the rest of humanity. Ordinary people, Robin. You may not have met them.'

'Not many Bristol owners, then.'

Unit 146 was a concrete structure surrounded by a high iron fence with a hoist alongside, as at the power station. It had on it the company logo and name but nothing else. Charles was already signalling to turn in when he cancelled and drove straight past. A white lorry was parked beneath the hoist, which was lowering on to the lorry's hydraulic ramp a square red container, sealed and with triangular radiation markings. As they passed they glimpsed a youngish, overweight man in the cab, slumped back in his seat and smoking, his elbow on the open window. The body of the lorry lowered as it took the weight of the container on its ramp. There was a small forklift nearby.

'Looks like we're too late,' said Robin.

'But it's not them. At least, they're not in sight. And we don't know for sure that that's it.' Charles stopped when they were out of sight round the corner. 'Why don't you walk in now, see what's happening? We'll wait here in case James is there after all and he sees us. Don't linger – if that is Deep Blue and it's going somewhere, we want to follow it.'

'Why do you want to follow it?' asked Sarah when Robin had gone.

'In case they hijack it. Or in case that was really them, pinching it.'

She stared at him. 'Charles, are you sure about this?'

'No. But we'll know one way or the other soon enough.'

'I don't understand why you're so determined, why you can't just leave it to the police. You've done everything you reasonably can. It's not because you've got some grudge against James, is it? Because he got away with it – or didn't get caught – last time?'

'No, it's not personal. Or not in that way, not with regard to James.' Charles fingered the wide, two-spoke steering wheel. 'It's sentimental, really, more because I – because of those two Russians who led us to the original plot. Both dead now, of course, so it makes no difference. But I feel that I owe it them somehow, we owe it to them, to take it seriously. They took what they did seriously. And if James's scheme works it could have enormous political consequences for the country. Not to mention lethal consequences if they cock it up.'

'I'm not sure your Russians would think this was a very serious way of going about it.'

Robin reappeared, walking briskly. He protested as Sarah transferred herself to the back of the car but Charles cut him short. He grinned as he buckled his seat-belt. 'That's it, that's what's in that container, Deep Blue. It's being put out to stud, going back to be replaced because it's tired out with all the work it's been doing, nearing its half-life. The new one comes in a couple of days. No sign of James or his oppo, just a driver.'

'Where's it going?'

'It's already gone.'

'So we've missed it?'

'Not quite.' Robin grinned again. 'I had a word with the driver on the way out. Asked him the way to Glasgow. He told me and I asked if I could follow him, pretending I thought he was going there. He said "No, mate, I'm going to Sellafield, you don't want to follow me there." Then he drove off. So we can look up the route to Sellafield and catch him up. Does that qualify me for MI6?'

'Sarah, is the road map under that stuff on the back seat?'

She sighed. 'What's the point of following it to Sellafield? It'll be out of harm's way there.'

'I want to make sure it gets there.'

'Sorry about this, Robin. Best humour him until he's back on the pills. I'll do the navigating, you do the pedals and steering.' She opened the atlas. 'Back on the A69 and head west.'

The road was busy with lorries that morning and they were not far short of Hexham when they saw the white lorry ahead. Charles stayed a couple of hundred yards back, sheltering behind one of Eddie Stobart's articulated forty-tonners.

'How will you know if it pulls off if you stay out of sight?' asked Robin.

'Watch and hope. I don't want to risk tucking in behind him until we have to. This car's too distinctive.'

'Told you we should have brought my Golf,' said Sarah, as their eyes met in the mirror. 'That has a satnav, too.'

It was a slow journey, which was just as well because

the car was running low on fuel. A truck in front prevented them seeing the white lorry pull off into the Little Chef until they were almost on it. Charles signalled right to turn into the Henshaw BP service station slightly beyond, on the other side of the road. 'I'll join the queue to fill up, you two get out and keep an eye on what he's doing.'

Sarah and Robin wandered back along the verge, feigning interest in the cattle in the adjacent field. Sarah leaned against the fence as they talked, which gave her a clear view of the Little Chef. 'He's parked in the corner,' she said. 'The driver's got out and is heading for the restaurant.'

'Hope he's not too long,' said Robin. 'Black and white cows aren't my favourite. They don't match the English countryside. Too stark. Cows should be brown or reddish brown or tan.'

'Two men have just come out from behind the trees in the corner. One of them is James, I'm almost sure. Don't look round.' She grabbed his arm. 'I said don't look now, they'll see you. They're getting in the cab. They must have keys or he left it unlocked.'

'Maybe they're pinching it.'

'The driver's coming back now with a bottle of something. Don't move, he's looking straight at us.' She glanced down at her feet. 'He's getting in the cab now, in the passenger door. It's reversing, they're leaving. We'd better tell Charles to stop filling up. Don't move yet, they're facing us.'

When the lorry was back on the A69 and heading west again they walked quickly back to the forecourt. Charles had reached the front of the queue and had just started to fill up. He stopped and replaced the nozzle. 'I'll have to pay for what I've had.'

'I'll do it.' Robin ran into the shop.

By the time they got back onto the far side of the A69, the white lorry was out of sight. 'I suppose you feel vindicated now,' said Sarah, smiling this time as their eyes met in the mirror.

Chapter Twenty-Three

The Present

'Use your bloody mirror!' Zac's tone was unusually assertive. He was still crouching in the footwell of the cab, trying to avoid contact with Rob's long legs. Rob was sitting in the middle seat and James was driving. The rear wheels had nudged the kerb. 'Change up, you're all right in top now,' said Zac. 'Just aim for a steady two thousand revs in whatever gear you're in.'

'Where's the . . . ? Oh yes, got it.' James sat upright, his arms almost straight at ten-to-two on the wheel, staring ahead as if pursuing a vision.

'Didn't drive like this on your HGV test, did you?' continued Zac.

'Never took it. Just had some lessons.'

'What if the police stop us, want to see your licence?' said Zac.

Rob's laugh was a mixture of bark and cough. 'That's really likely, that is. Stealing the most radioactive thing in Britain and they worry about your HGV licence. Is your passport up to date? What about your telly licence?'

Zac was silent for a few moments, before adding in a more muted tone, 'They stop you if you bash kerbs and things, 'specially HGVs.' There was another pause. 'OK if I come up now?'

'What's the matter, don't you like the smell of my trainers?' said Rob.

'Should be OK now,' said James, 'so long as you sit well back and don't thrust your mug at the cameras.'

At the M6, they turned north, trundling at a steady 60mph on to the M74 towards Glasgow. Conversation was sparse, a few remarks about places they passed or people who overtook them in luxury cars. Rob and Zac smoked, James relaxed a little, punctiliously flashing his headlights to signal to overtaking lorries that they could pull in. 'I could get used to this,' he said. 'More comfortable than cars.'

'Get bloody fed up with it, too,' said Zac.

They skirted south of Glasgow on the M8. Rob said they could call on his mother for a cup of tea. When they crossed the Erskine Bridge to head north and west on the A82, Zac said, 'What if the police stop us now, now we're heading for Faslane? They watch traffic round there, I bet. I bet they do.'

'Easy,' said Rob. 'Faslane is where we're going. That's why we're carrying a container with radiation warning signs all over it. They won't want to inspect that too closely, will they?'

'Where are you going to do it?' asked Zac. 'Drop it in the water.'

'Find a place when we get there,' said James.

'Can we stop for a piss?'

It turned out they all wanted one. Rob said he could do with a cuppa and something to eat. It turned out they all wanted that, too. But there was nowhere they could easily stop on the A82. James said they were bound to find somewhere when they turned off onto the A814 to Faslane. They passed a couple of cafés in Dumbarton but there was nowhere to park a lorry and James found negotiating the main street too stressful to drive off in search of somewhere.

'I wanna go, I wanna go soon,' said Zac as they left the town.

James pulled into a lay-by outside Dumbarton. A stone wall abutted the railway line, beyond which the Firth of Clyde stretched grey and sullen beneath broken cloud. They all got out and stood against the wall, where it was apparent that others had stood or squatted before. Two distant helicopters followed the line of hills behind them. Rob said the town on the other side of the firth was Greenock, where his grandparents used to live. Zac said he was famished. James said it wouldn't be long, they'd stop when they found somewhere.

Farther on, just before Cardross, they passed another lay-by occupied by a single car. 'That grey car,' said James. 'Don't know what it is but it's been behind

269

us since the M74 and it passed us when we stopped back there.' The others tried and failed to see it in the mirrors. 'It's old, whatever it is. Old registration.'

'They wouldn't use an old car for following us, would they?' said Rob.

'Who's "they"?' asked Zac.

'Anyone. Bloody Salvation Army for all we know.'

'It's behind us again,' said James after a while, his eye on the mirror. 'A long way back but it's there.'

'See if it's still with us after Helensburgh.'

It was. They were all nervous now, hunger forgotten. 'Pull off at the next turning and see if it follows us,' said Rob.

James shook his head. 'We're almost there. I don't want to start messing around, drawing attention to ourselves.'

'What are we going to do, then?' asked Zac, his voice slightly higher now.

'Keep on till we lose it.'

'How much fuel have we got?'

James hadn't thought about that. The needle was between a quarter and empty. 'Is there a garage at Faslane – Garelochhead, whatever it calls itself?'

'How do I know?'

Leaving Helesburgh and its wide seafront road, they passed the yacht club, a sign to the council offices and an outdoor pursuits centre. The loch-side was now shielded by a thick belt of trees which would have provided useful shelter had they not also denied access. Soon there was also a high wire fence and a barrier to the left, with a sign announcing the RN Clyde Base. On the right side of the road, half-hidden by a straggle of trees and undergrowth, was a cluster of garishly painted but unkempt caravans and ancient small coaches. A faded sign proclaimed the Faslane Peace Camp. James slowed, unsure what to do. He remembered the layout and size of Faslane from Google Earth but now, on the ground, it looked larger and less porous. They would have to get beyond it to find access to the water. The peace camp looked uninhabited. One of the more noticeable old caravans had NO DOVES FLY HERE painted across it.

'They crap here, though, I can tell you that,' said Rob. 'Gulls, anyway.'

'Where is everyone?' asked James.

'In London for the demo, most like.'

By the time they reached the Faslane South entrance the fence was topped with razor wire and monitored by cameras. Cranes, accommodation blocks and large industrial buildings were visible above the trees. After more miles of fencing and razor wire they came to the Faslane North entrance, where there was a roundabout and guards with automatic weapons inspecting vehicles queueing to enter.

'I don't like this,' said Zac, his voice squeaking at a higher pitch. 'All them police and military. And cameras, look. I might be on them.'

'Keep your hat on, we're not going in there,' said James, heading across the roundabout towards Garelochead. 'We'll only stop somewhere quiet. If necessary we can go round to Coulport on Loch Long, where they store the nuclear warheads.'

'I ain't going anywhere near them.'

'It might be better there, less built up. Also people will more likely believe in a radioactive leak where nuclear warheads are loaded and unloaded.'

'That car still following us?' asked Rob.

'Can't see it at the moment.' They passed a small filling station in Garelochead but he didn't want to stop, then thought he should have, then resolved that he would on the way back. All they had to do was find somewhere quiet for a few minutes, that's all it would take to unload. It was important to keep Zac sweet since they'd need him to operate the mechanism.

'We could've got some food at that filling station,' said Zac.

'Yeah, and something to drink,' said Rob.

'On the way back.'

After Garelochead, James turned left onto the B road leading to the Rosneath peninsula, keeping the water to their left. The road led around the peninsula to Coulport, loch-side all the way except for one section where it cut up inland. His hope became a determination that there was bound to be somewhere where they could unload Deep Blue swiftly and securely.

The dashboard now showed a yellow fuel warning light.

'We have to, there's no option,' said Charles as they pulled into the Shell filling station at the entrance to Helensburgh. 'Hardly got any in before.'

'Have they got many options on the road ahead?' asked Sarah.

'Not according to my phone,' said Robin. 'Unless they turn off right to Loch Lomond, which is hardly likely because no dead fish floating around there could be blamed on the subs. D'you think they've spotted us?'

'Probably,' said Charles. 'Should've. We're the only vehicle that's stayed with them.'

'This might reassure them, then.'

When he got back in after filling up, delayed by a uniformed naval officer who was curious about the Bristol and assured him that its battleship grey was wrongly named, Sarah and Robin were talking animatedly. Their words were drowned by the clatter of a helicopter taking off from somewhere ahead.

'Charles,' said Sarah as he pulled away. She leaned forward between the seats. 'We were just saying, while you were wasting time talking to that sailor about the car, that neither of us has any idea what we're going to do if we catch them. I mean, if they're in the act of tipping Deep Blue into the water, how do you propose to stop them? Wrest it from their hands and die of radiation poisoning a few minutes later? By which time they'd presumably be dead too.'

'They must have some plan for dumping it in its container without exposing themselves to it. Best thing we can do is watch where they put it so we can tell people.'

'But do we need to? Won't all the dead fish be a giveaway?'

'Ideally, we'd stop them doing it. Intervene before they dump it.'

'That's what I mean – by wresting it from them?'

'Ram your car against the back of the lorry so they can't get it out,' said Robin.

'There was a hotel back there, I'm dying to go to the loo,' said Sarah.

'Presumably you could claim it on expenses – the car?' said Robin.

Once again, Charles felt that no one – including half of himself – was taking this seriously. The outlandishness and amateurishness of the way James and his friends were going about it disguised the seriousness of its consequences, not to mention the physical dangers of a bungled operation. But he would pursue it to the end, whatever that was. Sentimental, perhaps, but he felt he owed it to Josef and Federov, brief and vivid tutors of his youth, the era of serious spies. The trail had begun with them.

Chapter Twenty-Four

The Present

'Where the hell are we? Nothing here but villas and bungalows for rich gits,' said Rob. After following the loch for miles without any vehicle access, with the cranes and moorings of the Faselane base just across the water, the road was now leading them inland. 'Not even a bloody puddle to drop Deep Blue in.'

'It's less built up farther on,' said James. 'After Kilcreggan, which is where we get back to the loch-side.'

'Yeah, but can we get to the water? Can't carry the bloody thing ourselves.'

'Bound to.'

'Sure, are you?'

There was an edge to James's voice that wasn't there before. 'I am.' James nodded without looking round, knowing he sounded more confident than he felt.

Eventually, they began to descend and the loch reappeared, at first intermittently, to their left. Beyond more bungalows and older villas in Kilcreggan, he slowed at a sign indicating a picnic area ahead. The trees thinned to reveal a few wooden tables and benches and signs announcing that deep water was dangerous.

'Be telling us it's bloody wet next,' said Rob.

'Could we reverse between those tables to the water's edge? Is there room?' asked James.

Zac craned his neck. 'Not with those minibuses.' Two minibuses from the outdoor pursuits centre were parked to one side. 'School buses, they look like. Don't want kids running round while you're unloading, do you?'

'No one in sight,' said Rob. 'Only take a few minutes.'

'They might come back.' James accelerated, conscious again of the low fuel indicator. They would have to find somewhere soon in order to have enough to get back to the filling station. At least the grey car was no longer with them; maybe it had turned off right for Loch Lomond.

Either side of the hamlet of Cove the road was as near to the loch as they could wish but with a sheer drop to the beach. The tide was out, which meant that the water was too far away for them to drop Deep Blue and its container into it. James didn't want to risk hanging around for hours, waiting for it to come in. If he'd thought about tides, they could have timed it differently.

'Christ!' exclaimed Zac, in his highest pitch yet.

He pointed ahead as they rounded a bend. Out in mid-channel was the sinister black bulk of a surfaced submarine. Accompanied by a sleek grey surface vessel, it was making its way up the loch, very slowly, with virtually no bow-wave. It rode high in the water and was much larger than they were prepared for. 'We can't do anything now, they'll see us.'

'We'll turn round, find somewhere,' said James.

'Reckon it's got nuclear bombs on board?' asked Rob.

'If it's a missile sub it might, if it's returning from patrol. Unless it's just starting and is going to load up.'

James wasn't unhappy that their attention should be distracted rather than focussed on their failure to find anywhere to dump Deep Blue. He was still looking for somewhere to turn round when, quite suddenly, the road ended at the entrance to the Coulport base. There was a mini-roundabout, the usual razor wire, great vertical slabs of rock and more armed guards, this time Marines as well as police. There was nothing else, no other vehicle, only a woman standing at a bus-stop. All the guards were looking at them. James edged the lorry gingerly round the roundabout and headed back the way they'd come. His heart was beating faster.

'We'll have another look at that picnic area,' he said.

'Where do they keep all the nuclear bombs and rockets?' asked Zac.

'In the rocks, stored underground.'

'Better not light a fag here, might get more than you bargain for,' said Zac.

Confident there was nothing behind him, James slowed to a crawl before reaching the picnic area. His caution was rewarded when he spotted a gap in the trees a hundred yards or so before the picnic area. They must have missed it before. It showed the land running level off the road with, at the water's edge, a small concrete slipway ahead, with no boats and plenty of room to pull off. James stopped and looked at Zac. 'Can you ... ?'

Zac nodded and opened the door. 'So long as the beach is firm enough.'

James and Rob walked on the beach, stamping, and stood by the slipway as Zac reversed the lorry towards it, holding up their hands when he reached it. Zac switched off and there was a loud hiss from the air brakes. Near-silence followed, apart from the lapping of the water and the cry of gulls. Zac climbed out of the cab. 'Want the forklift?'

'Can't do it without. And we need the doors open.'

'Do that yourselves.'

He threw them the key to the padlocks holding the bolts shut, then pressed buttons at the back of the lorry to lower the forklift on the ramp. As it lowered he looked across the loch. 'What if that submarine comes back and sees us?'

'It won't, it's going the other way.'

'Did you see all them guards with guns? They'd shoot us, no problem.'

'Just get on with it, will you?' said Rob.

The lorry's suspension eased as the forklift reached the ground. Zac climbed back into his cab.

'Aren't you going to move it, then?' called James.

Zac stuck his head out. 'Rob used to drive one, you said. He can do it.'

'Yeah, years ago,' said Rob. 'Not this sort.'

'Key's in it.'

Rob looked at James, mouthing obscenities. James shrugged. Rob mounted the forklift and after a minute or two of fiddling and looking, started it. He reversed off the ramp rather suddenly, laughed and then drove it forwards as fast as it would go, turning several times in front of the lorry and waving his finger at Zac in the cab, his hair flapping behind him. James unbolted the high doors and opened them wide. Inside was the solid-looking, dull-red, steel container, like an old-fashioned safe, standing on a wooden pallet and strapped to the floor. It was about five feet high but looked small in the back of the truck.

Rob looked at James. 'Get it out as is?'

James glanced at the empty road. There was nothing in sight. He nodded and released the straps. Rob raised the forks to the level of the pallet and eased his vehicle forward. He had to stop and adjust the fork height, then inched forward again until the blades slid into the pallet gap. He raised it carefully and reversed towards the top of the slipway until it was clear of the lorry. He lowered it until it was not quite on the ground. There were yellow radiation markings on the side of the container.

James raised his hand. 'Hold it there.' He walked around it. 'Can't see how it opens. The top must come off.'

'Ask him. He must've seen them do it.'

James went to the cab. Zac was smoking, his back against the door and his feet on the other seats. 'Can you show us how it opens?'

'I'm not coming out there with it open. I'm not coming anywhere near it.' He did not look round.

'We won't do it when you're there. Just show us.'

'I want my money first. You said half in advance and I ain't had any yet.'

James took a moment before saying, 'You can have it now, before we do it. As long as you show us.'

Zac sat up, threw the butt of his cigarette out of the window, climbed down and walked back with James to the forklift.

'He wants his money,' said James.

Rob looked from one to the other. 'What now, with this thing sitting here like this? Hadn't we better get on with it?'

'You said half in advance, half when we done it. You said.'

'For Christ's sake.' Rob looked at James, shrugged and got off the forklift. He felt in both back pockets of his jeans and handed two folded wads of notes to Zac. Zac stared at them without counting. 'It's all Scottish, it's all in Scottish.'

'Nothing wrong with that. Worth more because it's warmed by my arse. Now, come on, show us what to do. You can count it when you're on your bloody yacht. We want to get done and get out of here.'

Zac stuffed the wads into the inside pocket of his jerkin. 'You'll have to lower it right down.'

Rob remounted the forklift and lowered the container to the ground. Zac pointed to the square top. 'That's a lid, see? It comes off. You undo those four screws at the corners with that Allen key, see?' He pointed to a large Allen key slotted into a shaped groove in the centre of the lid beneath the raised handle. 'What I've seen them do, they take the screws out then lower it into water with a crane attached to that handle, then turn the handle with the crane and lift off. You'll have to do that yourselves. I ain't gonna hang around and watch, I'm going in the cab.'

They spent some minutes considering how to get it into the loch without exposing themselves to it. They had known this was a blank in their plans which couldn't be filled until they saw the problem. Best, they decided, was to remove the screws, turn the lid without lifting it, take it down the slipway on the forklift, then tip it into the water in the hope that the lid would come off and Deep Blue would slide out and do its work. They, meanwhile, would retreat up the slipway, shielded by the container.

It was the work of minutes to undo the screws and turn the handle a quarter turn until it stopped. 'Don't we wanna take the container away?' said Rob. 'Or they'll find it and know it's not the subs or the nukes or whatever.'

'But how could we get it out without going into the water and lifting it? It would be too heavy anyway, lined with concrete or something.' A breeze got up, ruffling the water and sending wavelets lapping against the slipway. There were distant sounds of a helicopter and, nearer, the voices of children from the trees farther on. James looked up. There was still no one in sight. 'We'll just have to leave it. They'll work out what it is quick enough, anyway, because this kind of radiation is different to anything that could come from nukes or subs, or so I've read. It just has to last long enough to make news in time for the demo tomorrow, and I can make sure of that. Then the campaign will be unstoppable. The government will deny it but no one will believe them. It's the panic factor we want, the hysteria, a lot of people frightened but no one dead, just a few fish. Come on.'

Rob's fingers rested on the ignition key. 'But if it tumbles out rather than just slides out it might zap us before we get far enough away.'

'Not if the container's between us and it.' James's anxious expression was at odds with his confident tone. 'Come on, we've got this far, let's do it and get back. The results will be worth it.'

Rob paused a moment longer, then turned the key. He raised the forks by a foot or so and turned on to the ramp, descending slowly. 'I'll get as far as I can into the water,' he shouted over his shoulder, 'but I don't want to stall it.'

'Remember we've got to get to it to push the container over.'

Neither noticed the dozen or so children who ran out of the trees away to their left, then stopped, looking on. Rob slowed as the slipway steepened. Like a flock of starlings after a pause, the children started making a noise again, shouting to each other. Rob looked round suddenly, inadvertently turning to the left. It wasn't much but enough for his front wheel to slip over the edge, causing the truck to bang down hard on its frame, rocking on the side of the slipway. The pallet, already steeply angled towards the loch, slid slowly off the forks. The container toppled with a crash on to the concrete, skidded a few feet and tipped into the water. The lid came off as it struck the concrete and a smaller, cylindrical container with flanges around it was thrown out. This stayed on the slipway, half-skidding, half-rolling into the shallow water, where it came to rest against one of its flanges. It had either never had, or had lost, its lid, and a lump of material about the size and shape of an overlarge house brick slid half out. Almost immediately the surrounding water began to turn blue.

After another, briefer, pause the children's excited shouting resumed as they ran towards the slipway.

Chapter Twenty-Five

The Present

After leaving the filling station, Charles never caught up with the lorry while it was still on the road. 'Shouldn't we at least try to let the police know what's happening?' asked Sarah. 'Seems irresponsible not to if we've lost the lorry.'

'OK, ring Bob.'

Bob's mobile and direct line were unanswered and the HQ switchboard would only leave a message for him to ring back. Then they lost signal. Charles pressed on, touching eighty on the straights and braking hard at corners or whenever they approached a possible pull-off place.

'I like this car,' said Robin. 'Let me know when you want to sell.'

'Have it now as far as I'm concerned,' said Sarah. 'Smells horribly of petrol in the back.'

Soon they were in the hills above Kilcreggan and

out of sight of the loch. 'Think they're making for Coulport?' asked Robin.

'There's nowhere else to go. Unless they find a convenient spot on the way. They just need to get the thing into the water without irradiating themselves. Doesn't matter where they do it so long as it's water used by the subs.'

'They could just drive the lorry into it and jump out.'

'No point if it's still in its container.'

'Slow down.' Robin spotted the picnic area and the minibuses before Charles. 'You'd think they might have tried that. Perhaps they've already done it.'

'Not enough room for the lorry.'

'There they are, look. There.' They passed the gap in the trees at sixty but there was just enough time to glimpse the lorry backed up to the slipway and three figures at the back with the forklift. 'Don't think they saw us,' said Robin. 'No one looked up. What are we going to do – go back and confront them?'

There was room to pull on to the verge after a couple of hundred yards. 'Any mobile signal here?' There was, but still no answer. Sarah left a message for Bob to call back. Charles was still undecided about the answer to Robin's question. What did confrontation mean – a fight, a chase, exposure of them all to Deep Blue? The answer was a recce, surely. A recce was nearly always best, looking before leaping, acting in the light of knowledge rather than the darkness of ignorance. 'We'll leave the car here and nip back and see what they're up to. We may be able to stop them dumping it but if we're too late and they've got away at least we'll know where Deep Blue is and it can be recovered before it does too much damage. Through the woods, not the road.'

They all three set off through the birch trees, which were not too dense and allowed for rapid walking. Sarah switched her phone to silent but kept it in her hand. They soon heard and then glimpsed through the trees a long line of children walking with two or three adults in parallel off to their right, along the shoreline. 'Keep away from them,' said Charles quietly, 'but their noise is useful cover.' They quickened their pace.

They paused just inside the trees, about forty yards from the lorry, in time to see the forklift almost tip over and the container bounce from the slipway into the water, bursting open. The man on the forklift jumped off and ran out of sight the other side of the lorry. The other one, James, ran towards the intersection of the trees and road, where they had paused. The lorry started and its rear wheels span, spurting sand and stones as it headed slowly for the road, revving loudly. At that moment, Charles saw that the leading half dozen or so children had burst out of the trees by the shoreline and were running towards the slipway, calling and shouting.

Afterwards, he allowed it to be said that he had reacted instinctively, since people found it an acceptable

ALAN JUDD

explanation for rashness. But he knew it wasn't only that; there was calculation, too. He shouted to Robin and Sarah to ring 999 and stay where they were, then ran towards the slipway. Absurdly – and this truly was instinctive – he half waved to James as they sprinted past each other, James fleeing Deep Blue and Charles heading for it. He ran between the children and the slipway, shouting and gesturing to them to keep back. They stopped and stared, silent now and open-mouthed. He saw the spreading blue in the water as soon as he reached the slipway. Only once there was he conscious of thinking. It mattered least that he should die: he was the oldest, it was partly his doing, the end would be quick, his internal organs failing or erupting in an overwhelming storm of alpha radiation. The thing was to act now, while he still could. If he could get it into deeper water there was less chance it would harm anyone on shore. He walked deliberately down the slipway to the upturned container, the restless ever-bluer water up to his knees. Resisting the impulse to take off his tweed jacket and roll up his shirtsleeves, he stooped and picked up Deep Blue. For a moment he imagined he was back in childhood, with his mother scolding him for getting his sleeves wet again. It was heavy, much heavier than it looked, and not blue at all when lifted clear of the water, just a dull grey-black. Balancing it in one hand, he bent sideways like a shot-putter and heaved it as far out as he could. There was a gratifying splash and then nothing.

He stood looking at where it had disappeared, waiting to feel. To feel what? He had no idea. Perhaps he would simply black out. Above the loch a great flock of gulls headed right to left, going seawards. The breeze had stiffened and the wavelets lapped faster. Blacking out would be a good way to go. Upsetting for Sarah but at least she would be out of it. The water was cold. He turned to wave goodbye.

Sarah and Robin were shepherding the children back into the trees, their backs to him, Sarah holding her mobile to her ear. The lorry, its ramp still down and its open rear doors swinging, was pulling on to the road back towards Garelochead, leaving the forklift behind. Next his ears were filled with a great noise, a clattering roar. A sustained blast of warm air almost unbalanced him. For half a second he thought this was it, this was dying, before turning to see a helicopter rounding the nearest trees and skimming across the water towards him. It was so low that he crouched, his thighs and backside in the water. As it passed overhead its wind buffeted him sideways, leaving him sitting in the water and struggling to right himself against the slope of the slipway. The helicopter landed on the beach where the lorry had been, disgorging helmeted uniformed figures with POLICE SCOTLAND emblazoned across their backs. As its engine and rotors wound down there were sounds of sirens from the road and flashing blue lights showing through the birches. Charles crawled up the slipway, soaked through now and wondering if he would be able to stand when he got there.

He could, albeit that he felt weak and unreal. He assumed this was the onset of radiation poisoning, but would otherwise have put it down to cold. Uniformed figures were up by the road in two clusters either side of the entrance. An older man in civilian clothes was rather cautiously descending the short ladder from the helicopter. To his left, the entire party of children and teachers were gathered by the trees, looking on. Robin was talking to one of the teachers and Sarah was walking towards the slipway, smiling and waving at the man leaving the helicopter. No one seemed hurried or bothered.

'That was brave,' she said, 'and very, very foolish. You must be freezing. Maybe you can have a bath in that hotel in Faslane and I'll buy some clothes, if there's anywhere that sells any. Or you could borrow a navy uniform. I'd like to see you in uniform.' She laughed and kissed him. 'Ugh, you are cold.'

Charles, as puzzled as he was relieved by her flippancy, almost gave in to indignation 'You shouldn't be here, it's dangerous, you should stay up by the road. And the children—'

She tugged at his wet jacket sleeve. 'Calm down, it's all right, it's not dangerous, or not any more. It never was, it turns out.'

'What do you mean?'

She nodded at the man from the helicopter, who

was walking towards them, grinning. 'Bob will tell you.'

Bob Shea held out his hand. 'Owe you an apology, Charles. Not just for making you take a cold swim but for letting you run off on another wild-goose chase. Remember I took a call when you were in my office? It was from MI5, Simon Mall. Seems they'd decided to take this thing seriously after all. He had the good grace to say you'd alerted them to it but didn't know you were off trying to sort it out yourself, running your own little operation up here. Said he'd tried to contact you but your office said you were on leave on a walking holiday in Northumbria, out of contact. When I said you were sipping coffee in my office he said to say nothing, to leave you be, wanted to tell you himself. Don't think he thought you'd get very far with what you were doing, though if he'd asked me I could've told him you wouldn't let it go, not after our earlier escapade. You had a score to settle.' He laughed. 'Better come and get dry. I'm sure they can sort something out back at the base, even if it's only wetsuit and flippers.'

Charles didn't move. 'But Deep Blue, it's still out there, it's—'

'Deep Blue's safe at Sellafield where it belongs. What our merry men hijacked was a harmless substitute packed with dye. We didn't even have to follow them till they got up here, thanks to the tracker in the lorry.'

'So the demo tomorrow ...'

'Our friends won't be attending, sad for them.

It'll be two short. Nor will there be any sensational announcements about nuclear warheads poisoning the whole of Scotland. All's well that ends well, eh?' He laughed again and clapped Charles on the shoulder. 'Let's get you back to your car. Unless you want a lift back with our friends?'

Up at the road, James, Rob and Zac, all handcuffed, were being helped into separate police cars. James looked round just before the policeman holding him pushed his head down to get in the car. For a long moment he and Charles stared at each other.

'It's OK, I'll drive,' said Charles.

'*I'll* drive,' said Sarah, determinedly.

Chapter Twenty-Six

The Present

Elspeth Jones sat in the Windsor chair now placed among the sofas and armchairs in the Foreign Secretary's office. She was a short woman and the leather club seating that had served for years made it embarrassingly difficult for her to sit with her feet on the floor. Also, the Windsor chair meant that she sat higher than everyone else. She placed her teacup delicately back in its saucer.

'It's really Robin you should thank,' she told Charles. 'He spotted the loophole, or at least persuaded the Chancellor's SPADS that there was one. So you have agreement in principle to move, you just need to find a building.'

'And you think Victoria Street is now taken?'

'It's not clear,' said Robin. 'We'll know in a couple of weeks. Meanwhile, the important thing is, your request to leave Croydon is on paper as having been formally agreed before the Chancellor's ban on further moves. The fact that it wasn't until I wrote that post-dated piece of paper is neither here nor there now that it's been accepted, since no one will look at it again.' He smiled across the rim of his cup. 'It's only putting on paper what had been orally promised anyway. It's too trivial for the Chancellor to bother with and every-one's happy except Melanie Stokes, late of this parish.'

Melanie had resigned in the wake of the Deep Blue revelations. Charles realised he was probably alone in feeling any sympathy for her. Ambitious and self-seeking, certainly, but she wasn't the only one in that world; she fought her corner, was loyal to those she was close to, didn't kiss-and-tell. The day the story broke it was clear she was under threat: James's media profile and links to Triple A ensured widespread cov-erage of his arrest and plot. Her twin positions as James's partner and adviser to the Home Secretary with responsibility for security matters gave the story legs and within a couple of days the Opposition was asking in Parliament about her role as his 'close and long-term confidante', calling for an inquiry into the circumstances of her appointment. Once the Home Secretary became part of the story, there was no doubt she would have to go; she resigned promptly, giving no interviews and putting the bare minimum on social media.

Coverage then shifted to the plot itself, with specula-tion about the consequences had it worked, the extent to which it was known about by others in the Triple

A leadership and even a reference to James's role in its forerunner many years ago. Gratifyingly, there was no mention of Charles, which was what convinced him that Robin was the source. By the weekend, all that was left for the Sunday papers and TV and radio analysis was fearful examination of the little-known role of radioactivity in cleansing and preserving vegetables and salads, causing predictable outrage in sections of the population. When the fuss died down, he thought, he would buy Melanie lunch.

'The police and MI5 came out of it well, gratifyingly for the Home Secretary,' said Elspeth with a small smile. 'And, equally gratifyingly, you seem to have kept yourself and MI6 out of it, Charles.' She turned her smile to Robin. 'A low profile makes the office move a little easier to handle. And now, with the Triple A discredited and the Opposition forced to distance itself from them, it's easier for us all to get on with representing and securing the interests of this still-United Kingdom.' She turned back to Charles. 'Thank you, Charles, and well done. Shows it pays to be persistent. Sometimes.'

Afterwards, on the stairs, Robin produced from his pocket a white envelope. 'The proposal form for membership of your club. I've completed all the CV bits, you just have to add your paragraph of unstinting praise and sign it. No need to find a seconder. Turns out I was at Cambridge with the club secretary's son.

We had a good chat when I called in to get this. He'll find a tame committee member to second me. Hope you don't mind.'

For a moment, Charles hesitated, but only for long enough to consider what Josef and Federov would have done. They would never have hesitated. What to him felt like a compromise, albeit a minor one, would to them have been an incomprehensible scruple. The goal had been achieved, the bad prevented, the good ensured. It would be unseemly to quibble. He took the envelope. The feeling of being manoeuvred, if not quite outmanoeuvred, was novel. And the man had demonstrated he could be a useful ally in Whitehall. If survival was success, it was built on compromise. He smiled. 'Look forward to seeing you there, Robin. Come and have a drink.'

Alan Judd is a novelist and biographer who has previously served in the army and at the Foreign Office. Chosen as one of the original twenty Best Young British Novelists, he subsequently won the Royal Society of Literature's Winifred Holtby Award, the Heinemann Award and the Guardian Fiction Award; he was also shortlisted for the Westminster Prize. Two of his novels, *Breed of Heroes* and *Legacy*, were filmed for the BBC and a third, *The Kaiser's Kiss*, has just been filmed as *The Exception*, starring Christopher Plummer and Lily James. Alan Judd had reviewed widely, was a comment writer for the *Daily Telegraph* and writes the motoring column for *The Oldie*.